MW01109484

ANGEL
A HUSTLING DIVA
with A TWIST

ANGEL

A HUSTLING DIVA

with A TWIST

ANGEL'S RETIREMENT
BRENDA WRIGHT

AuthorHouse™
1663 Liberty Drive
Bloomington, IN 47403
www.authorhouse.com
Phone: 1-800-839-8640

Published by AuthorHouse   01/22/2013

ISBN: 978-1-4772-8615-9 (sc)
ISBN: 978-1-4772-8613-5 (e)

Library of Congress Control Number: 2012920718

Any people depicted in stock imagery provided by Thinkstock are models, and such images are being used for illustrative purposes only.
Certain stock imagery © Thinkstock.

This book is printed on acid-free paper.

Because of the dynamic nature of the Internet, any web addresses or links contained in this book may have changed since publication and may no longer be valid. The views expressed in this work are solely those of the author and do not necessarily reflect the views of the publisher, and the publisher hereby disclaims any responsibility for them.

Acknowldgements

I want to thank god first for guiding me in my quest to write, and second I want to thank everyone that have supported me along the way you know who you are. I want to thank my husband for his support in holding my hand every step of the way, thank you baby, and my grandchildren, you guys have been great in helping me send e-mails and giving me quiet time when I needed it thanks for having my back love you all, and for all my readers, thanks for supporting me in my journey to write by purchasing my books I can only hope that you guys enjoy reading Angel as much as I did in writing her, I hope my readers found the complexity of reading about Angel entertaining. With Much Love Brenda Wright.

chapter one

King's Birthday Bash

—— •◦• ——

King was celebrating his nineth birthday Dallas was getting club sophistication ready for a surprise birthday bash for king he was even flying in some exotic strippers from Hawaii for the event, king wasn't really tripping off having a birthday bash he was more interested in his girlfriend Aphrodite she had young king nose opened wide enough to drive a fifty seven Chevy straight up his nose, King called Aphrodite to setup some dinner plans when she declined only because Dallas had informed her that they were throwing King a birthday bash at club sophistication, when she told king she wasn't going to be able to make it to dinner he wanted to know why so she told him because she had already made other arrangements king told Aphrodite that was fine and that he would catch up with her later on she said cool kissed king good bye and close her front door behind king.

King couldn't believe that Aphrodite had turned him down they were thick as thieves together so for her to dismiss him was making king think something was going on with her, what king didn't know was Aphrodite was preparing for his big birthday bash she wasn't dismissing him on purpose she was just helping Dallas and baby girl get things ready for king's birthday bash, king was so pissed at the fact that his girl didn't want to spend time with him when he wanted her to until he went to club sexy to have a few drinks, every drink he took made him angrier by the minute only to find out later by a big mouth trick name Royal that he was having a birthday bash at club sophistication at eight that night, king thought to himself oh wow now I know why my girl was acting so suspect with a nigga she know how to keep a secret I think she's a keeper for real.

The party was in full swing when Dallas and his brothers Diego, and Detroit came in the door with King he was smiling like a pimp at a players ball he wasn't surprised but he couldn't tell anyone that the trick Royal told him that they were throwing him a birthday bash, when king looked to his left and seen his girl standing there wearing a long silk cream colored Jennifer Lopez designer sequence gown he was about to past out she was looking like she just stepped off America top model runway she was gorgeous and king made sure he told his girl that she was stunning, after king thanked everyone for his birthday bash he took Aphrodite by the hand and lead her to the dance floor for a little bump and grind king was enjoying himself until a big fight broke out right in the middle of the dance floor, a guy was swinging on another guy when someone threw a bottle and hit king upside the head king was furious he escorted his girl off the dance floor out of harm's way, he returned to the fight in the middle of the floor and started swinging on people his soldiers followed suit when one guy got pissed because he got punched in the mouth he pulled out his 9mm and started shooting up the place, people were running all over the place people were getting stampede trying to reach the front entrance to club sophistication.

While the guy was shooting up club sophistication king was outside the club with his soldiers killing up his Westside enemies they spotted king when he came in the door but king didn't think twice about them Westside cats because he had all twenty of his soldiers watching his back, one nigga in particular that didn't like king young ass was this nigga name do dirty he couldn't believe that king tried to run him off his block he wanted king dealt with but king had put the word out that he was now that man that ran the whole Chicago area and if a nigga had a problem with it come holler at him, the word did spread like wild flowers king had built up a lot of enemies in a short time but he didn't give a damn he was the king and he wanted to let every drug dealer know who the king was.

King and Aphrodite was on their way to the mall when his driver spotted a black Tahoe following them he wanted to make sure that the SUV was really following them so he asked the driver to make a few turns to see if his imagination was playing tricks on him, and to his surprise he was right the guys that was following king was trying to force them into a ditch they drew their guns only to find out young king had bullet proof windows, when the two guys failed to penetrate kings car king henchmen Dallas and Detroit started firing at the two guys car striking their gas tank until the car exploited the only thing you could see was black smoke escaping from their car, the two guys went up in smoke with their car when the fire department got to the scene the only thing they saw was just the frame of a burning car the guys bodies was just a memory of what was in the car from the wittiness that saw what happen, but the wittiness wasn't able to tell the police that king was responsible for what happen because they knew young king pulled a lot of weight and they didn't want to be his next victims so they kept quite.

King had other ideas for him and his sister baby girl to take their
stacking paper cartel to another level his thoughts of being the
kingpin of his cartel was at a all time high king was already a
multimillionaire he was getting the big head and was enjoying the
thrill of it all, baby girl was so busy with so many cases until she
realized that she hadn't spent know time with her brother since
his birthday bash so she was just about to call king when he came
strutting through her office front door, she stepped from around her
desk to give her brother king a hug when she noticed he had this
weird expression on his face she asked him what was wrong? When he
asked her if they could have dinner together so they could talk about
a few things, she agreed to meet up with him at her place at seven
kings smiled and accepted her proposal to be at her house at seven.

King had a proposition for his sister that he didn't know for sure that
she would go for but he was going to try his hand with it anyway
and if she didn't go for it he was going to just drop it, king had been
feeling good lately he had falling in love with the woman of his
dreams he had all his soldiers in line and he had just purchased his
first home at the age of nineteen, his house was a three million dollar
home with seven bedrooms five bathrooms a nice open floor plan
with a big kitchen with all stainless steel appliances with a three car
garage, king also had marble floors in all his rooms was decorated
with Italian furniture with antique statues he had wall paintings of
Malcolm X, Martin Luther king, Maya Angelo, Diahann Carroll, Nat
King COLE and rappers like Tupac and biggie smalls known as the
notorious B.I.G. king had his crib setup just like the king tower he
had his shit on lock.

King made it to his sister's house at six fifty six he was always punctual when it came to the women in his life he didn't want to disappoint them by being rude.

When king made it to his sister's front door all he could smell was this fried chicken aroma coming from the cracks of her door baby girl had fried chicken, Mac and cheese, candy yams, with some baby lima beans with cornbread muffins she had a small spread waiting for her and her brother, it was finally time for them to sit down to a soul food dinner for a change, king told his sister if you wasn't my sister I would marry you in a heartbeat they looked at each other and broke out laughing like crazy, baby girl asked king what would he want to drink he asked baby girl you know I think I want something I haven't had in a while she asked him what's that, king said some kool-laid they started laughing again because king would always show his teenage side to his sister but around everyone else his mannerism was tough and rugged king carried the power of twenty men, baby girl asked her brother king to join her in her den for their conversation she wanted to know what her little brother had up his sleeves this time.

King started his conversation off by telling his sister he loved her she commented by saying I love you too, so what's on your mine little brother I'm dying to know what's going on in that head of yours, king started to run down the proposition he had in mind for his sister king wanted to wash up a lot of money through his sisters law firm to open up some legal business for a studio for some talented rappers he knew he also wanted to buy a whole strip mall with another club inside the strip mall, baby girl had to think for a minute because her little brother already had as much money as any young man of his age had ever seen she saw were king was getting a little greedy so she knew she was going to have to slow his role for him before he self destruct, when baby girl told king that she would give it some though he automatically knew she wasn't falling victim to his shit, before king decided to leave his sister's house he told baby girl that he was sorry that he shouldn't have asked her to put her law firm in jeopardy for him because he wanted to wash up his illegal money, baby girl told king to hold up maybe we can come up with a way that we can wash up your money and we both can benefit from the transaction.

Baby girl told king to give her a couple of days to handle some things and she would get back with him he said alright and went out the door, when king made it to his car he didn't see the dark blue sedan sitting across the street from his sister's house watching him it was two detectives name Tim Taylor and Mark Beckham they were assigned to follow king from their commander and chief because king name had been ringing like a elementary school bell, detective Taylor wasn't about to pull king over for the stop light he just ran to him they had bigger fish to fry and king was prime rib they weren't taking any chance on botching up their assignment on no damn traffic violation.

King was driving alone the freeway bobbing his head to one of tupac's songs hell Mary he didn't have a scared bone in his body he didn't fear anyone in his mine everyone feared him, king pulled into the service station when he notice the dark sedan pull over to the side of the road he called his sister to let her know just in case he got pulled him over, she told king to give her the license plate number so she could run it through her topnotch computer system to find out who they really were, when king hung up the phone baby girl started her investigation and found out that her brother was being followed by detectives Taylor and Beckham, her inside man that worked for the feds told her everything she needed to know that her topnotch computer couldn't, when Donnie told baby girl that king was on their high alert list she got a little nervous because she knew her brother was dirty without a doubt but he never even had a parking ticket, when baby girl call king to let him know what was up and that he needed to chill for a minute until she could look into things to see what they really had on him he said alright sis that's what's up let me know as soon as you find out alright, baby girl said alright and king drove around for a while until he could lose the two detectives that was hot on his trail.

King drove up to the Mac Donald's just to throw the detectives off but they wasn't having it detective Taylor didn't like drug dealers especially those who rode around town in 100,000 dollars cars, so king looked suspect to detective Taylor, king was a target he wanted king young ass sitting in jail or on death row for all he cared he told his partner that if it was left up to him he would have king locked up in a cage like a monkey until he died, right then and there detective Beckham knew his partner not only didn't like drug dealers he was a racist period he didn't know why his captain hadn't pick up on it, when king went in the fast food restaurant the two detectives got out their car and stood next to kings candy apple red Lamborghini, even thou Beckham was mixed with Cherokee and white he still felt that Taylor ass was wrong as two left shoes and he made sure Taylor felt what he had to say about the statement he made about young king.

King came out to his car just in time because Taylor was shining a flashlight through his car window to see if king had any drugs in his expensive ass car so he could arrest king and have his car towed, king not only had a sister that was a kick ass attorney he knew his rights they had no apparent reason to follow king up in the restaurant or harass him at all, officer Taylor was told to follow him not harass him and that's actually what he was doing harassing young king jeopardizing whatever case they may have against king, when king asked Taylor why was he looking in his car without permission Taylor punched king right in the face he only added fuel to the fire now king had the right to sue the police department for assault and harassment charges, king requested to go to the hospital to get his face looked at because his eye started to swell on impact, Taylor told king he didn't need to go to the damn hospital and that he needed to spend some time behind bars for two ounces of cocaine he found on the ground near his right tire of his car.

Taylor told king you can either go home or go to the hospital king told detective Taylor fuck you I want to go to the hospital because your punk ass going to pay for putting your damn hands on me without a cause I have wittiness's that just saw you hit me in my face for nothing, when detective Taylor looked up it was four people with their cell phones out taking pictures of the incident, those people that saw what happen didn't even know king they didn't know if he sold drugs or not but they did see what happen to him they had pictures on their phones to show that detective Taylor hit king for no reason, he had just walked up to his car to get in when detective Taylor stepped in front of king to stop him from getting in his own car.

chapter two

Gloria (Baby Girl) And Steven Fighting The System

———————•●•———————

Baby girl got a call from a nurse in the hospital emergency room reporting that her brother Ramon king Carter was admitted to the hospital for bad abrasions to his face, his eye had completely close from the punch he took in the face from detective Taylor the nurse couldn't believe that detective Taylor was a racist he didn't try to hide how he felt once he made it to the hospital he was screaming all kinds of obscenities, everyone in the waiting area was in a uproar his partner tried to get him to calm down but he wasn't having it detective Taylor was acting like he had lost his damn mine, his partner detective Beckham had only been his partner for three months because his other partner had gotten killed in a drug bust gone bad by some teenage drug dealers, the sting that was setup for them to kick in on went sour because the soldiers they had on the roof top seen the activities from the roof they sent word that the cops were on the block kicking in doors and they were headed their way once detective Taylor partner Cody got out of his car he got hit with a 9mm holding hollow point bullets piercing his bullet proof vest, detective Cody died on the scene and detective Taylor hadn't been the same since they had been partners for ten years, when the nurse requested that detective Taylor be removed from the hospital he was very upset his partner Beckham call their captain to let him know that detective Taylor had finally broke down he had lost his mine in a public environment everyone seen and heard his racism tactics he was way out of line.

Baby girl rushed to the hospital to see her brother laid up in the hospital with a swollen eye he also had abrasions to his right jaw, when baby girl seen what her brother looked like she lost it he was swollen like a NFL football on a football field being kicked by one of the players, baby girl went straight into attorney mode she was going to sue Chicago police department for every penny she could get, she first found out from all four wittiness what happen she talked with them all she also had the pictures from their cell phones to show what happen to king, she went into her office and drew up papers for police brutality against her brother and police harassment charges she knew she wasn't going to be able to defend her brother because of conflict of interest, baby girl decided to call her boyfriend Steven to put him on the case but she wanted to work silently alongside Steven on this case which she thought would be in her and her brothers best interest, baby girl called Steven and he came to her side he dealt with the cops on a daily basics so he knew just how to handle the case with kid gloves, he had just came off a case with a cop beating a fifteen year old boy that he beat to death so this was right up his alley to string a cop up for excessive force, this was another brutality case that Steven was more than happy to help get the compensation they needed.

Steven had personally handled a lot of sexual harassment cases along with numerous police brutality case's he successfully won at least ten of them, Steven called what they did to king was conscious and deliberate action he also stated that Taylor publicly with fury about his racism, baby girl really wanted to go public with the case she want NAACP aware of what was going on, police brutality may occur violating the rights and liberties of any individuals, Steven knew baby girl was right in standing up for the rights of her brother but he also knew that baby girl are her brother didn't need the publicity that they were going to get with contacting NAACP or the civil rights movement, he wanted her to think about what she was saying he knew she was angry but she had to put her anger in prospective because for one her brother was a drug lord kingpin.

Steven asked baby girl to sleep on what she was thinking and if she still wanted to involve the NAACP and the civil rights movement then so be it, but he wouldn't advise her to do so they had too much at stake, after baby girl left the hospital she had calm down a lot but she was still pissed at the thought that detective Taylor put his hand on her brother, king got released from the hospital the next morning he stopped by his sister house him and Dallas, Diego and Detroit with him they all agreed to sue the police department without the high profile publicity and after they settle up with the police department they were going to take Taylor out of his misery for good he wasn't going to be around to let anyone else know he was a racist pig.

Steven went to his office and drew up some more form's to start the ball to rolling on prosecuting the Chicago police department while he was there he thought that he would stop in and say a few words to the new police commissioner Johnny Newhart, when he knocked on the commissioners door he said come in when he looked up and seen Steven he was smiling from ear to ear quiet as kept the new commissioner was Stevens Uncle, so to make the trial go easy Steven thought that he would call in a few favors from his Uncle when he asked his uncle for advice on how to pull a trick out his bag without taking the uncle down with the police department his uncle told him I have a lot to tell you about that asshole Taylor he's been a threat to this department for a while I knew it would be just a matter of time before he crossed the line, first nephew let me tell you something I'm put this bug in your ear but you didn't hear it from me alright Steven told his uncle he wouldn't intentionally involve him with anything, commissioner Newhart told Steven that the whole department knew that Taylor was a racist he should have been removed from the department years ago when he killed a young Hispanic guy in a jail cell doing questioning in the interrogation room last year, yes internal affairs investigated the incident but they pushed some shit under the rug because I heard that he was questioning the young man without him being handcuffed to the chair the young man grabbed Taylors gun him and Taylor got into a wrestling match the gun went off and shot the young man in the heart, plus when the shit hit the fan about the detective killing a young man doing questioning didn't anyone mention the fact that the young man had took a beaten from Taylor before the incident even happen.

Steven told his Uncle he heard about that case and he too thought that it was some shady shit going down because the only thing happen to Taylor was suspension without pay doing the time internal affairs was investigating the case, but this time Stevens uncle the commissioner was going to help Steven get Taylor ass out of the department and off the streets he wasn't going to let Taylor think that because he had a badge he could take the law in his own hands and do what the hell he wanted to do Taylor had became a street vigilante with a badge and a gun, Steven knew his uncle was definitely on point with what he was saying about Taylor because from the pictures he seen on baby girl cell phone of how Taylor punched king in his face with full force and didn't show any sign of remorse was a clear sign of police brutality, Steven left his uncles office with a new profound attitude he knew he had detective Taylor by the ball's not only was he going to bring down Taylor he was going to bring down the police department and internal affairs for allowing Taylor to still be on the police force knowing he was a racist and he didn't have any emotional physiological help after the death of his former partner detective Cody.

Steven had the trial date set for three weeks he want to get this over and done with quick he didn't want to drag the case on for years he really wanted them to settle out of court that way he could string their ass up for the murder of that Hispanic young man family as well, because he didn't think that the young man's mother didn't have her day in court to get vindicated for her son's murder, she never had a real reason to what happen to her son only thing she could find out was her son was responsible for his own death by snatching the gun off of detective Taylors side, the police kept trying to justify arguments of evidence that her son had been beaten before detective Taylor pulled him over with a gun under his seat, the real reason detective Taylor pulled the young man over was because he was swerving his car from lane to lane the young man was high off heroine he was incoherent at the time he couldn't even remember driving his car at all, Steven wanted to find some closure for the young man's mother so, he found out who she was from digging up the case records he called Mrs. Martinez when he told her who he was and what he wanted to do for her she cried because now she could rest at night and she would have peace to know that she could get justice for the death of her son, king couldn't sleep at nights because he wanted detective Taylor so bad it made his dick hard he wanted to show him what torcher felt like for real, the case date was coming up fast and Steven had all his ducks in a row he had all four wittiness to the king case he didn't think he needed the pictures he even had detective Beckham as a wittiness, so he knew his case was going to be a slam dunk Steven even had his kick ass attorney baby girl as his silent partner sitting at his side so he was straight, Steven had one week left before the trial began king's swollen eye had went down but he still had a little red in his eye he also had the pictures that the emergency room doctor had took of his face just in case Steven needed them. Detective Taylor was still watching king he had it bad for him, he felt in his mine that if king hadn't went to the hospital he wouldn't be going to trial he thought to himself I should have killed that drug dealing bitch why I had him hemmed up at Mac Donald's.

The trial has began and every wittiness that were subpoena showed up including detective Beckham he was getting eyes from every officer that was there in the court room they couldn't believe he turned on a fellow officer, what they didn't know was they didn't see detective Taylor in rear form he was slobbing at the mouth like a pit—bull in heat, he had so much hatred in him that he couldn't control his actions detective Beckham wasn't the only one to see detective Taylor act out his racism in a public environment other officers had seen him get crazy on more than one occasion, when Steven walked up in the court room everyone got really quite they wanted to hear what the police department had to say about their police department using excessive force on minorities' and specially on king because he only walked out of Mac Donald's with a hamburger and a coke went to his car Detective Taylor stood in front of king stopping him from getting in his car the next thing everyone seen was detective Taylor punching young king in the face, Steven had never seen a trial go so fast they settle quick because they knew Taylor was a for real ass hole king was rewarded three million dollars for the police brutality case plus he got another million for pain and suffering for his eye.

Gloria a.k.a. baby girl didn't have to do nothing but sit back and watch her man work, Steven had that shit wrapped up and sewed up they never even seen it coming he came in the courtroom ready baby that nigga was sharp as a tack, he had his shit together and the Chicago police department knew to fold the hell up.

Taylor got fired from duty the next day he was never going to be a police detective anywhere in the world again Steven still had unfinished business with the Chicago police department he was still going after them for the death of Mrs. Martinez son Tony Martinez.

chapter three

The Killing Of Detective Taylor

——— •●• ———

After the trial ended king stuck to his word about taking Taylor out of his environment he wanted to make him feel all the pain and suffering he took him through and anyone else that ever crossed paths with detective Taylor, Taylor was so upset about getting fired he was out for revenge he thought that he was going to be watching king this one night in particular but he was too drunk to leave home, when he was sitting in his living room drinking like a fish when he heard noise coming from his kitchen, Taylor reached on the table in front of him to retrieve his pistol when he realized he was stripped from his weapon and badge from the police department the day he got fired.

Taylor was scared shitless he grabbed a vase from his shelf and started to the kitchen in a slow motion stride he wanted to surprise whoever the fool was in his house trying to rob a cop, then it dawn on him that he's not a detective or a cop anymore so he had to do what he had to too protect himself he went down his long hallway that lead to the kitchen when he step to the kitchen door Diego sprayed some mace in his face.

Taylor dropped the vase immediately and started rubbing his eyes that's when Dallas hit Taylor across the head with his own vase and knocked him buck out, Dallas and Diego picked Taylor up and carried his limp body to their car and threw him in the trunk of their

car when they reached the warehouse Taylor was still knocked out
from the blow to the head that Dallas gave him, Dallas gave king
a call to let him know that his packaged had arrived as plan he was
grinning because he knew he was going to set fire to that ass as soon
as he reached the warehouse king wanted to do something to Taylor
that he seen in a porno movie. so he went in his backyard to get his
Rottweiler's he had two of the meanest Rottweiler's a nigga ever seen
they did shit on command whatever king said they did, king put
his dog's in the car and headed to the warehouse when he pulled up
Diego and Dallas started smiling because they knew king was about
to do some real treacherous shit because he only would bring the dogs
out when he had some treacherous shit going on in that head of his,
king got out his car and asked Dallas where was that piece of shit
Taylor he told king he was still knocked out tied up to the high beam
they had in the ceiling, when king walked in the warehouse he looked
at Taylor he said out loud wake your racist ass up look at me because
I'm going to be the last person you see before I turn my dog's a loose
on your trifling ass, Taylor looked up at king and said you can kiss
my whit Lilly ass before I bow down to your punk ass I might suffer
from your hands and that's alright because I will meet your ass in hell
you can bet your life on that, king was so pissed after what Taylor said
to him he took a switch blade out his pocket and cut Taylor straight
across his forehead cutting it wide open he looked at his dogs and
said attack, they jumped on Taylor ripping his ass to shreds they were
tearing parts off Taylor like he was a side of beef at a packing house
he didn't even have time to holler out because they was on his ass like
flies on shit.

Once the dogs was done ripping Taylor a new asshole literally it wasn't nothing left but blood it looked like my bloody valentine massacre had took place in the warehouse, king called his cleaning crew out to clean up the blood that was in the warehouse he also needed the dogs cleaned up as well they looked like they had been to a raw meat festival, king was happy that Taylor ass was gone for good he wasn't even worried about the cops looking for him for Taylor's disappearance because in reality didn't know one on the police force wanted anything to do with Taylors racist ass.

It had been a couple of weeks before anyone notice that Taylor hadn't been seen around town when his only friend Jessie went to check in on him he really didn't like the fact that Taylor was a racist but they were long time childhood friends, Jessie went to Taylors house twice in one day only to hear his neighbor say I haven't seen Taylor in a couple weeks the last time I seen him he walked outside one morning two weeks ago to retrieve his news paper that's the last time I seen him, Jessie decided to use his emergency key to Taylors house to get in when he open the door he was in a state of shock he started vomiting instantly, king made sure that he wanted Taylors balls in a vise grip twist for real king is definitely his mother angels child when Jessie seen a pair of balls twisted up inside a pair of vise grips hanging from Taylors bedroom mirror like a pair of hanging dice he started vomiting all over again, Jessie called the police for assistance they took their time getting to Taylors house when Jessie called but when they got their to see what Jessie had found they didn't have much to say because Taylor deserved everything that happen to him.

Baby girl was glad that Taylor got what he deserved she just hated she wasn't a part of his demise, king was back on his grind again he was stacking paper almost as high as Donald trump, king was pulling in a million a month on king towers alone he was sitting pretty on his other two drug house as well but things was bothering young king he started letting that money go to his head the more he made the more power he processed, king really though that he was the king for real he thought he couldn't be touched by the long arm of the law until Taylor showed him he can now that detective Taylor is gone he stepped his stacking paper game up to another level, king started interviewing girls for his drug trafficking ring he thought that the police will check nigga's on the freeway quicker than women so he decided that his trafficking ring would consist of females only, king interview ten hard looking females before he decided that if he had bitches that looked harder than men they would get pulled over for looking harder than a nigga, so he said to himself fuck that if I'm make this work I'm going to need some eye candy and still keep my butch looking bitch'es for bodyguards for my eye candy.

King hired six exotic females for his drug trafficking business he also had six big female bodyguards to protect his eye candy and drugs, king was getting shipments of drugs from uncle Leo and flying some of his eye candy out on drug assignments, he had three of them along with their bodyguards driving across state lines going all over the country to pick up his drugs the women wasn't scared at all because they had criminal records they had been introduced to king from his sister baby girl, she was literally recruiting female criminals from her attorney files she was an attorney but she was also a female assassin like her mother angel as well, baby girl had took being an attorney to a different level she was using her criminal skills to recruit criminals from her selected list of criminals, baby girl now has a feline list of female soldiers along with drug runners she along with her brother king has opened up more business's since king moved to Chicago than their mother ever did.

They even has a warehouse full of antique cars that they put in car shows for sell king has at least four 123, 0000 dollar cars he's putting up for sell in their car show, what young king don't know is the feds has flagged him he soon will be getting a visit from them very soon, he has a snitch in his camp because envy is a bitch and the green eyed monster don't have no friends trust and believe.

chapter four

Baby Girl Playing Both Sides Of The Fence

———————————•◦•———————————

Gloria a.k.a. baby girl knew she was playing too close to the fence when she decided to start recruiting clients from her files she was taking chances that could not only send her to jail for the rest of her life but she could get disbarred from ever being attorney anywhere in the world, she was so use to running things her way until she forgot the fact that her best friends Ava and Denise was a part of the law firm as well, what affected the law firm affected them too even thou they didn't mind what she did as long as she kept them in the loop and lately she been spending so much time with Steven and king she really hadn't thought to much about her partners and it was starting to get old real quick, Ava came in the office the next morning to find Denise sitting there going through some files she told Ava that we have some problems I think we should talk about, she asked Ava did she know that baby girl was recruiting female criminals from their cases to run drugs up and down the coast for king, Ava looked at Denise like she was talking in tongue she said I didn't know about any of this until now, so we need to get baby girls ass in this office for a discussion before we all be behind bars, do you really want to cross swords with angel's seed because you know that bitch is a one woman killing machine like her mother you know as quite as kept I think angel was responsible for the disappearance of Abby and Gabriel we can't prove it but all the signs are there.

Baby girl was listening to Ava and Denise's conversation they were so deep in thoughts of talking about her that they didn't notice her standing in the hall right by the door, she knew one day that the subject of Abby and Gabriel's disappearance would come back and bite her in the ass but she really didn't have anything to do with the killings but she did have knowledge to what did happen to them, when baby girl decided she heard enough she pushed the door open Ava and Denise looked like they had seen a ghost they really wanted to know how long she had been standing there and how much she heard them say but they didn't have the guts to ask her, baby girl knew she had been spending a lot of time away from her friends but she thought that they friendship was strong enough for her girls to understand the rules they had set in place in case either one of them had gotten into a relationship. when baby girl talked to Ava and Denise they had squashed being mad at her for neglecting their friendship so they made plans to hang out after work, what baby girl couldn't get off her mind was the fact that they were holding court on her about what they had just found out about her criminal activities concerning recruiting females they were defending in court on drug cases, baby girl was beginning to feel a little lonesome she was missing her mother she wanted to talk some things over with her about what her and king had been doing but she knew it wasn't know way possible for her to reach her where she was living, she just wanted her mother to know that her and king had things under control while she was gone and they were keeping the family business running as plan.

Baby girl and her girlfriends meet up at club sexy after work they were sitting at the bar drinking absolute and cranny berry juice when they were approached by these four guys claiming to be drug dealers but didn't neither one of them have baller status, see what they didn't understand was baby girl and her girlfriends knew all about drug dealers it's a difference between being a drug dealer and a baller, ballers carry deep pockets they deal with heavy weight were as drug dealers have corners and niggas selling rocks for them while they brag about what the other nigga's doing for them, ballers have bragging rights they have bitches, cars, houses, and heavy money to back their shit up some of them even have they own business's the only thing about messing with a baller is competition is furious as far as the ladies goes you talking about big dick with little heads they only think with their dicks not with their brains.

Baby girl decided to let Ava and Denise in on the new scheme her and king had going on it wasn't that she wasn't going to tell them they just happen to find out before she told them, when she invited them in on it they were all good but baby girl still wanted king to know that her girls was part of the family and it was only right for all of them to be smart in the decisions that was going to made between them for now on, baby girl happen to be going into court one day when she saw Steven talking to the commissioner in the hallway by the elevator they were in a deep conversation because he didn't even notice her come in the side door, she already felt that they were hiding something from her but Steven never changed how he treated her so she was alright with it for the time being, but what puzzled her the most was how could Steven not tell her he had a personal relationship going on with the commissioner, so she decide that when she went home for the evening she would boot up her lap top to investigate the new commissioner Newhart, later that day Steven gave baby girl a call so he could come over for some much needed stress reliever every time Steven would start feeling tension he would call baby girl for one of their lovemaking sex sessions that would calm his nerves a lot, but this particular night she didn't want any company she was too busy trying to find out why Steven and the commissioner were so damn close her antennas would go up every time she would see the two of them in deep conversations with each other, even thou Steven didn't know everything about her business's she still wasn't sure about letting him into her heart just yet, plus baby girl still wasn't sure she wanted a man she really didn't know around her son.

Baby girl was amazed at what she found about the new commissioner Newhart he was related to Steven on his father's side of the family, he was Stevens uncle and Steven forgot to give her the memo that sent up red flags in baby girls book because Steven came to her she wasn't trying to have a relationship with him at first she didn't even know he existed until he walked into her office, once baby girl found out that Steven was hiding the fact that his uncle was the commissioner she wanted to know what else was Steven hiding so she decide to check his ass out to she thought she would rather be safe than sorry, when she started checking out Steven's background she found out that Steven was married with children he had an office in Atlanta and in Chicago his wife and children lived in Atlanta, she was sitting at her lap top in a state of shock she said this nigga is playing with my emotions and I'm going to fuck him up, baby girl dug a little deeper to find out not only was Steven married they had pictures of him and his wife and children wrote up in magazines in front of a big ass estate, she didn't want her feeling to go no deeper than they had already gone for Steven so she thought she should cut her ties now before he regretted what she was going to do to him.

Baby girl didn't want to admit it but her feelings was already past emotional she felt Steven in more ways than one, baby girl just said to herself she would just keep her distance from Steven for now but he will pay for lying to her and leading her on, baby girl had two new case she was getting ready to try in court it was a case about two Cubans that had smuggled four key loads of cocaine into Chicago on a boat it was hidden inside a dead alligator that they said they caught in a fishing net both men claim the alligator was already dead, but couldn't explain to the authorities how the alligators stomach was split wide open with none of his organs, they were arrested with fifty thousand dollar bonds and held into their court dates due to them skipping out of town, baby girl like the two Cuban guys she thought to herself that these two were the kind of guys her and king needed on their team if they were bold enough to split open an alligator and take out his organs and fill his guts with drugs then they were alright in her book plus the two Cubans had heart, baby girl was going to get them released by all means necessary she felt deep down that they could use them for gutting a nigga if nothing else.

Baby girl son Cane a.k.a. Smoke had gotten to the age where he was skipping school hanging out with nigga's that was twice his age he had gotten into a car theft stealing ring, even though he loved his uncle king he also envy the fact that king was stacking paper hand over fist he had gotten so jealous of king he started selling drugs in one of kings spots which he knew was a no no, he also knew that king name rang volume in the streets didn't know one dare cross king everywhere that smoke went he heard somebody talking about king like he was god, that made smoke angry even thou he had everything money could buy he wanted what king had the power to make people do whatever he wanted, Smoke was so upset with king beaming with stardom until he was beginning to hate he even knew king he couldn't even have peace in school because all the fast ass little girl's wanted to bed king in ways smoke had only heard of he never had sex before but he thought that now would be as good of time as any since the ladies know him as being kings nephew that would be to his advantage to get in some panties, baby girl happen to be with a client when her private line started to ring it was the principle at smoke's school calling about her son smoke he hadn't been to school in three days, baby girl went straight off on the principle because she couldn't believe that it took them three days to inform her that her son had been absent for three days before they notified her.

Gloria (baby girl) made plans to go up to the school to see what the hell was going on she didn't tell smoke she was coming she was going to surprise him by visiting him at school without him knowing or was smoke going to surprise his mother baby girl by not showing up, when smoke got up on Tuesday morning getting dressed for school he took a shower got dressed ate breakfast kissed his mother good-bye and headed out the door for school, what smoke didn't know was his mother knew how to pick up signs and follow you like a grey hound she was on to smoke the minute he walked into the kitchen as soon as he made it out the door she was hot on his trail, baby girl followed her son to a beat up garage on fifth avenue he slid up the door and went in, what she saw next shocked the shit out of her she seen at least six nigga's sanding and repainting cars, the cars looked to be stolen cars but baby girl wasn't sure but she knew that her son didn't need to be around those guys when he should have been his ass at school, baby girl knew that she had to do the unthinkable to get her son's attention so she put in a call to the police to let them know where to find the stolen cars and the perpetrators, she really wasn't sure if they were stolen but she did know that they all looked suspect including her son.

Baby girl didn't want to involve the police she just wanted to scare her son straight even thou she knew she was crocked as hell herself, she wanted better for her son but she knew one day he was going to get caught up in the madness of the family business she wanted him to finish school go to college and get a degree in accounting, baby girl sat down the street when the police raided the garage when she seen them bring out her son in handcuffs she got queasy as hell because he looked like the bird who ate the canary, baby girl went back to her office to wait on a phone call from her son she knew for sure he wasn't going to be able to lie his way out of this lie he was about to tell her, when the phone did ring it was the police that had arrested her son he told baby girl that her son was arrested for car theft and tampering with stolen cars, she asked the officer did he have a bond and the officer told her his bond was fifteen thousand dollars secure which means she had to pay fifteen thousand dollars in cash or use her home as a property bond, she told the officer that she wasn't going to come and get him out tonight but she would be there to pick him up the next day she wanted him to feel how it felt to be caged up like a animal, what baby girl didn't know was smoke begin in jail over night wasn't going to change him he had been locked up over night before when she let him stay all night at his friend Joey house, Joey's father was the ring leader he was part of them stealing cars and tagging them and selling them, smoke and the other guys knew not to ever mention who ran the car ring to anyone and they stuck to keeping manic a secret he wasn't mention as of yet, baby girl didn't give a damn she was going to find out who had her fourteen year old son stealing cars and tagging them, when baby girl went to get smoke the next day he couldn't look at his mother he dropped his head she told smoke look at me your ass is in a great deal of trouble so you are going to tell me exact ally what's going on or I'm going to take your little ass right back into that police station and leave you there to let them do what they see fit for your car stealing ass so what it's going to be.

Smoke told his mother who manic was he told her that he was his friends Joey father he also told her where he stayed, baby girl was pissed she was going to see this manic person because he had really stepped out of bounds she was going to set fire to his ass about her son, when baby girl showed up at Maniac's house he couldn't believe that smoke snitched to his mom he knew that baby girl wasn't know joke because she defended him in a drug case but she didn't know him as maniac she knew him as Joseph Phillips, when Maniac told baby girl what was really going on she was totally pissed because maniac tried to flip the scrip he told baby girl that her son was the leader of the car stealing ring and they was working for him, baby girl said you know what that's some bull shit and you know it but this the last time you will ever see my son and anyone else's son far as that matters, Maniac told baby girl bitch I'm maniac who the fuck you think you talking to I don't give a damn about your punk ass brother king yeah I know he suppose to be the man I know all about his young ass, maniac was walking up on baby girl drooling from the mouth like a dog that has rabies before he could get any closer baby girl stepped back reached in her purse and pulled out her 45 and put two right between Maniac eyes he was laying on the floor with his eyes wide open baby girl bent over and spit right in his face and said you shouldn't have fucked with my son you stupid bastard.

chapter five

Steven Taking On The Chicago Police Department

———————•●•———————

Steven had been reading the case file on the murder of a young Hispanic guy that been arrested and murder by detective Taylor while being in the interrogation room being questioned by Taylor, Steven gathered all the information he could on the death of Tony Martinez before he contacted his mother to let her know he was taking her case probono he wanted MRS. Martinez to have her day in court for the death of her only son, while Steven was looking through the files something happen to fall out of an envelope it was about five picture of Tony Martinez his face looked like he had been three rounds with Mike Tyson, it amazed Steven because he had gazed at the files on his way to court that morning but he didn't remember seeing any photos in no envelope when he looked real good at the photo's of Tony Martinez there was a lot of bruises on his face and neck that no one seem to mention in the reports, Steven said to himself that it was some suspicious shit going on in the police department and internal affairs that needed to be addressed A.S.A.P. before Steven took steps to contact Mrs. Martinez he wanted to first fine out who in the hell put the photos in his files, then all of a sudden it hit Steven like a ton of bricks he remembered his uncle the commissioner telling him that he would help him hang the Chicago police department and internal affairs for letting detective Taylor get away with the murder of Tony Martinez, Steven knew he was going to try his best to keep his uncle from getting caught up in this case he was getting ready to fight, he was going to do his best to give Mrs. Martinez some closure for her son.

While Steven was down at the court building he stop in at the clerk's office to pull the police procedures and manual he was pulling out all the stops on this case he wanted some heads to roll and he damn sure wasn't going to stop until he got Mrs. Martinez some answers, he left the clerk's office and headed back to his law firm Steven was so excited until he forgot he hadn't ate lunch until his secretary knocked on his door to let Steven know she was calling domino's for a pizza he told Diane that she could order him a turkey sandwich with Swiss cheese, Steven stayed late that night at his office because he had enough evidence to bury the Chicago police department, now it was time to give Mrs. Martinez a call so he could get the law suit going Steven knew it was too late to call Mrs. Martinez it was after ten but with news like he had to tell her his heart wouldn't let him wait he wanted to expose those dirty ass cops much sooner than later, the next morning Steven was back in his office at eight thirty reading over some of the police procedures he knew the procedures but wasn't nothing wrong with getting back into the books he thought to himself, he would read the police procedures and he would look at the police reports he had on Tony Martinez he couldn't believe that everyone in the police station was crooked how could they let one of their Detectives beat a young man as bad as he did Tony Martinez and not do some kind of disciplinary action it wasn't even wrote up in any of the reports.

Steven called to setup a meeting with a judge to make sure his case
will be heard by someone that wasn't dirty, once Steven talked with
judge Murphy and he explained everything that had took place
judge Murphy was more than ready to hear both side's so Steven
had a court date filed against the Chicago police department and
internal affairs, he had two weeks to prepare his opening statements
and he was more than ready to hang their assess out to dry, he even
found out through his uncle the commissioner that detective Taylor
didn't even read Tony Martinez his memorandum rights, he only
pulled him over because he was swerving his car from lane to lane
only to find out Tony had lit a cigarette drop it between his legs
while he was driving he was only trying to get the cigarette from
between his legs, when detective Taylor and his partner Beckham
pulled up on Tony Taylor didn't ask for Tony driver licenses or his
insurance card he Just asked tony had he been drinking and before
Tony could respond to detective Taylors question he just started
hitting and kicking Tony like he was mad at the world his partner
tried to stop him but he kept breaking free from the hold detective
Beckham had him in.

Detective Beckham knew that Taylor was committing police brutality
on Tony he act like he was out of his mine sometimes for real, and
Beckham wasn't going to let Taylor take him down with him so after
they put Tony in their car he told Taylor that you really need to get
your shit together because you're headed for a whole lot of trouble
and I'm not going to be a part of it partner or not my job is all I have
and I be dam if I'm going to let your crazy ass get me fired on some
bull-shit, once Taylor and his partner made it to the station with
Tony Martinez everyone at the front desk checked Tony out they were

looking at him because they all knew Taylor was a loose cannon and they knew one day Taylor was going to cross the line and have the whole station in question, that day has finally arrived and the first person Steven wants to cross examine is detective Beckham because he was with Taylor the night Tony Martinez got pulled over until they took him into the station.

Steven knew once he started the case in court it would bring publicity he wanted everyone involved to be in partial compliance, Steven knew the law so it didn't hurt to brush up on the curriculum, he knew one thing for sure that the memorandum of agreements between the city and U.S. department of justice needs to be terminated with the police department being in full compliance with 93% of terms and conditions.

Steven was going to make sure he got them back to where they belong and also make his self look good in doing so; he wanted to make a request in to the city's commitment to minimizing the risk of police brutality in the Chicago police department and to promote police integrity, also for the department of justice to do investigations with the city and Chicago police officials leaders of the fraternal order of police sentinel police association, community members and civil rights organization representatives, training curriculum, supervisory procedures and Disciplinary system.

Steven was going to speak on memorandum rights also called for an independent monitor to continually be assessing progress, and for the city to present a regular status reports to be monitor, as well as the citizen complaint authority, to achieve full compliance, Steven knew he had to have all his ducks in a row dealing with the city because they had shark ass attorneys just like him so he had to dot every I and cross all his T's, for as Steven was concern they all needed to be under a microscope, Steven was so caught up in suing the city that he had put some of his own clients on hold so he could take on the city for Mrs. Martinez he had a week to get his shit together for trial, he really wasn't worried because he had everything he needed and then some he was so enthused with this whole scenario that he knew he could prove without a shadow of a doubt that Taylor killed Tony Martinez.

Steven opening statement would start off with (the violence must stop) the message is communicated through a number of different mechanisms we have to wake up people we can't tell the street gangs that they need to stop the violence when we have vigilante cops doing killings right inside the police station that double standards isn't it? What we going to do tell people do as I say but don't do what you see me do, homicide is at a all time high in the Chicago area we as the people has to take the initiative and save our people especially the young people we have to let them know that consequences will be delivered to the people who continue to engage in violence no matter who they are justice will be served.

Steven knew his opening statement will set fire to the people involved because he was right on the money it wasn't anything they could do to detective Taylor because he was dead but the city of Chicago had to answer for their misconduct to Tony Martinez and that was a true fact, Steven court date had finally came he sent his driver Wyatt to pick up Mrs. Martinez he wanted her there front and center, when Mrs. Martinez arrived Steven had just called detective Beckham to the wittiness stand he was just getting sworn in to tell the truth and nothing but the truth, Steven had pictures that was taking at the time of Tony alleged beating from detective Taylor that he found out later the night before the trial that they came from detective Beckham cell phone, when he started questioning detective Beckham about the evening they pulled Tony Martinez over he told Steven what happen from the time they stopped Tony until the time they made it into the station for interrogation, detective Beckham also told Steven that everyone on the force knew that detective Taylor was a force to be reckon with he even said he think some of the officers was afraid of Taylor, Steven went on to ask detective Beckham was he afraid of Taylor? He said sure because at times it seemed like Taylor would have out of body experiences I would have to shake him literally out of the daze he would be in, alright detective let me ask you this did you ever go to your superior about the way detective Taylor was acting? Yes but it was like it went on deaf ears because Taylor was right back doing the same thing I don't think my captain even called Taylor in his office to speak to him about his behavior until the incident with Mr. Martinez, so in other words you're telling the court that your superior didn't advise detective Taylor he wasn't in compliance? Detective Beckham answer with a no.

The trial went on for three days with Steven questioning each officer that was on duty the night of Tony Martinez death, everyone that Steven questioned had the same answer about detective Taylor even thou Taylor was dead they hung his ass out to dry so in reality Taylor committed murder right inside the police station interrogation room, the judge had heard enough he found the Chicago police department liable for the Murder of Tony Martinez and awarded Mrs. Martinez two million dollars for the death of her son and another million for pain and suffering. Mrs. Martinez was happy she cried the whole time holding on to Steven she wasn't crying because they won the case she cried because now she could finally have some closure, but the money will help with buying her son a head stone to put on his grave it wasn't right to Mrs. Martinez that the police had killed her only child they made Tony just another number laying in the cemetery and that she would never forget, Mrs. Martinez thanked Steven from the bottom of her heart for taking on her case but she told Steven she couldn't stay in a place that treated her so cold and if she stayed in Chicago it would be detrimental to her heath. Mrs. Martinez moved out of Chicago two months later to move in with her sister in Texas Steven told Mrs. Martinez to stay in touch and he would do the same.

———————————— •●• ————————————

chapter six

Ava And Denise Newfound Love

———— •◦• ————

Ava and Denise was spending a lot of time partying after work both girls were beginning to get lonely they wanted someone to hold them at night, one night in particular they went to club sexy and in walked two identical twin brothers name Kaylen and Keith they were two fine ass brothers kaylen was a little darker than Keith with smooth chocolate skin when he smiled he could bright up a room and Keith had the same smile both brothers had enough swagger going on to represent them all by its self, they were dressed to impress they both were wearing Versace shirts with black Versace slacks and they had enough jewelry on to choke a horse them to brothers were into some shady shit you could tell just by looking at them, but Ava and Denise liked the rugged edge the two brother possess.

Kaylen notice that they were being watched so he tapped his brother on the arm to let him know that a couple of honeys was peeping them Keith said alright let's make this easy on them lets go buy them a drink and entertain their thought's, Kaylen was the smooth talking one he slid over in a chair right next to Denise she was smiling like a chipmunk looking for a nut, Keith on the other hand is a hard core nigga with an attitude it's either his way or the highway type of nigga just the type of nigga Ava likes somebody that has a hard side like she does, three drinks later Ava and Keith was ready to bounce she had eyes for him and he was feeling her in ways she only dreamed of he was going to make it happen and Ava was more than happy to oblige him because she hadn't had her back cracked in months so she wasn't about to past up the opportunity to satisfy her sexual appetite.

Kaylen and Denise on the other hand was taking their time getting to know one another Denise all of a sudden started getting hot a bothered so she asked Kaylen if he wanted to go back to her place for a night cap, Kaylen told Denise hell yeah I'm in like Flynn let's do the dam thing baby I'm cool with whatever you want to do lets bounce, that night was like bombs going off in both apartments Ava was rocking Keith world he never had a female to turn his young ass out she had that nigga calling her name in tongue he knew right then and there that Ava was a keeper she wasn't about to take his young ass to heaven and call it quits.

Kaylen on the other hand was a passionate lover he took his time with Denise she was like m&m she melted in his mouth, Denise didn't know what hit her she was squirming under his touch like her life depended on it she was falling for Kaylen quick, they made slow and sensual sex all night while on the other had Keith and Ava was going into overdrive only this time Keith flip the scrip on Ava's ass she wasn't looking for him to put her ass in a twister stale mate position for those who don't know what I'm talking about imagine having sex at the same time, you talking about burning some serious calories the woman sitting in a chair with both feet planted on the floor, with her arms wrapped around the man, the man is on his hands and knees we all know how difficult a twister can be that position there will either break that ass or make you jump off a fucking cliff.

Now that Kaylen feels that he has Denise feeling more comfortable in his sex charades he know it's time to take it up a notch, he learned this wheelbarrow trick while he was spending time with his cousins in Jamaica it's just like a childhood game, the woman places her palms on the floor, facing away from the man, he then stands behind the woman, lifting up her lower body by the front of her thighs it's like a for real wheelbarrow race, I could go on and on with the different positions but I think I will stop here.

Denise and AVA meet up the next morning for breakfast they couldn't stop talking about the sexual activities they had the night before they both were very fascinating by the two twin brothers Kaylen and Keith, what Denise and Ava didn't know was Kaylen and Keith were hired guns sent to murder king by this Jamaican nigga name Jasper he was Buddha's brother, Buddha was the one who had the street shoot out with king and his soldiers, Jasper son got killed in the shoot out and Buddha got killed by kings corrupted cops but they made the setup look like king killed Buddha, Kaylen and Keith came strapped they had some heavy artillery they even had their car special made to carry some of their artillery, they had a custom made2011 mustang yellow & black with the front bumper carrying 2 Thomason guns, 2 mk. 40, 2-40. mm with extended clips w/ lasers pointers, CZ 75 Automatics extended clips w/ laser pointers, in the back bumper they had mp.13, with mp 40 submachine guns, they also carried a suitcase that held Jamaican bombs with two 45 hand guns with extra clips, they had been hired to kill king but one thing they knew for sure was when they got ready to run up on king they needed to be ready because they had been hearing king name ring in the streets since they arrived in Chicago.

Later on that day the brothers decided to go peep out king towers they wanted to get some escape routes down on paper so they wouldn't get caught tripping, they also wanted to get some more updated pictures on king the pictures they had of king was kind of blurry so they had to rent a car because they didn't want their mustang to get recognized by anyone other than Denise and Ava, when Kaylen and Keith pulled up on kings block they both said in unison this little nigga stay in the hood he got this bitch locked the hell up, Keith told Kaylen hold up man let's see how many soldiers this nigga got because we going to have to him them fast and hard, Kaylen told Keith you know we are going to have to do this shit soon because we know retaliation is a bitch I didn't come all the way from Jamaica to get sent back with no dam tag on my toe aight, silence fail on both brothers while they were sitting down the street from king towers Keith was ready to make king towers crimson red, while Kaylen was sitting there thinking of a master plan he wanted to make sure they had a full proof plan.

Denise was at work thinking hard about Kaylen he put some shit on that ass she couldn't even function she thought that she finally found someone that could handle that ass, so in the back of her mine she knew he would be her man so she thought what her and Ava didn't know was they didn't really come to Chicago to have relationship they had been following Denise and Ava for almost two weeks, Jasper did his homework on king and anybody else that was associated with king so Denise and Ava was just a porn caught up in jaspers little plan, it was time for Kaylen and Keith to kick shit in gear they heard from Ava that king was throwing a celebration at club sexy for his sisters birthday so to them that would be the perfect time to get a real view of king and his soldiers that way they would have their target in eye view for sure.

Club Sexy was off the hook the night of baby girl's birthday celebration it was people of class up inside the club it was lawyers, bankers, politicians, judges, and police officers so everybody that was somebody was invited to kick it with baby girl for her party even the commissioner showed up, but like always the hood nigga's always show up with that hood shit and spoil everything dam thing, it was a nigga name speedy that had just got into town two weeks ago he had four big nigga's he met in New York that he paid to be his bodyguards he was a big time drug dealer his self, so he thought he could come to Chicago and run king ass up off his set he had another thing coming he was going to need more than four big burley ass nigga's to shut king down, when Kaylen and Keith seen speedy come in the door with these big four muscular ass nigga a light went off in their head they looked at each other and said this shit might be easier than we think all we have to do is start some shit between king and that nigga sitting over there eyeballing our target.

Kaylen said you might be right my brother all we have to do is put word out on the street that king is looking for any nigga that thinks he's bad enough to go up against him for his territory, and then in return we will hire a bitch to go tell speedy that king is telling people that he need to take his country ass back to New York before he get's shipped back in a wooden box, the brothers started putting shit in motion that night and it wasn't long before they started seeing the fruits of their labor, shit was flying around in the streets about speedy and king like flies on shit and king was more than ready to step to speedy about his name coming out his mouth.

Mean while the brothers were still getting their freak on with Ava and Denise they was so caught up in the mystery of being hired killers for the Jamaican nigga Jasper that they hadn't paid attention to the fact that Jasper was watching their every move, one thing Jasper said was I give them there props on the bitches they picked up two bad ass bitches but that's not what I sent them here for, they're here to collect retribution on the death of my son and brother, Jasper sat outside Ava's apartment getting extremely pissed because in his book business before bitches was his model he wasn't trying to see it any other way, Ava started hearing rumors about the two brothers a couple days later she couldn't believe she let her being Horney override her senses the rumors that she heard was the two brother were hired killers what she didn't hear was why they were there in the windy city.

Ava decided to give Denise a call to tell her about the rumors that was floating around about the brothers so they called Kaylen and Keith to invite them to dinner to see if the rumors were true or was it just speculation, Keith being the strong headed person that he was he wasn't going to lie because he was sent there to do a job not play house nigga with no bitch so he was going to tell her what she wanted to hear, Kaylen on the other hand he didn't like hurting females feeling but when it came to his job a bitch would have to stand in line because killing was what the brothers did for a living and wasn't nothing or no one coming between them and their paper.

When the brothers told Ava and Denise that they were hired killers they really wasn't distraught because they had been having so much bad luck when it came to men so it wasn't a surprise to them but the sex was off the chain, Keith was just hoping they didn't ask them who were they sent to Chicago to kill but in reality Ava and Denise knew it probably was king because he had Chicago locked down, and he had killed people from some of everywhere that came at him wrong so why was it any different than the two brother going after him to.

Keith and Kaylen had a couple of days before they went up against king so they were locking and loading up their artillery, Keith cell phone started ringing when he notice it was Jasper calling he told his brother that Jasper was about to be itch in his ass, he said after we take this nigga king out we going to put Jasper ass to sleep to, Kaylen told Keith you tripping now because that nigga owes up a grip so if you want to kill that nigga go head but I want my money first player, Keith told Kaylen if you think I'm kill his bitch ass without getting paid first you crazy as hell nigga step back I got this stop tripping man damn.

———— •●• ————

chapter seven

King All The Way Live!

———————— •●• ————————

King got up the next morning full of energy he was going to take
Aphrodite on a shopping spree at the mall like he promised her but
in the same token he had a real bad itch that needed to be scratch,
he couldn't get the thought out of his mine about this new cat
name speedy that's been singling him out so as soon as he was done
shopping he was going to drop his gal off and get his soldiers so they
could go pay speedy an up close and personal visit it was time to see
what was up with his arch enemy, king was the type of nigga that
didn't take threats from anybody he was more like a hands on type of
nigga if you had something to say then king will come to you to hear
what you had to say.

While king and his soldiers were gearing up to go find speedy the
twins Kaylen and Keith was watching shit unfold right before their
eyes they were thinking maybe they could kill all kings soldiers and
take king and hang his ass from a roof top, when king got a funny
feeling that he was been watched he told his three right hand men
Diego and his two brothers Dallas and Detroit that he had this weird
feeling that it's some strange shit about to go down and he had a
feeling they were going to be right in the middle of it so they had to
be very cautious.

When king rolled up on speedy and his bodyguards he didn't know what the hell was going on until king jumped out the car with his soldiers with all their weapons drawn, he grabbed speedy by the neck he told speedy I hear you want to see me nigga so what's on your mind? Speedy said first of all young blood I'm not trying to kick off no shit, I was told you want me to take my country ass back to New York so what's the deal? King told speedy look we men nigga that's some bitch shit you trying to pull I'm a man straight up if I'm looking for your ass trust and believe you on my radar player, king was so in tune with speedy it fuck him up that a nigga like king carried so much power king made him feel like an ass hole he checked speedy drawers up his ass in front of everybody, king told speedy if you want to live nigga be the hell up out my city before sun rise and that's not a threat that's a promise homie.

When king snap his fingers his soldiers fell in line they loaded back up inside their hummers and headed back to king towers, king told Dallas if that pussy ass nigga is not gone by sunrise I want him chopped the fuck down, king was still feeling like he was being watch so he made a mental note to himself to check his perimeter's as soon as he made it back to king towers because his antennas never went up unless something was out of whack, as soon as king made it to king towers he went straight into his camera room he knew he wasn't getting those funny feeling for nothing he ran his cameras back for three days because it was best to be safe than sorry, only this time the camera only showed this guy that king knew he looked very familiar to him but he couldn't put the face with the young man's body form when all of a sudden it hit him, king started hollering ole snap that's my nigga Cisco from Columbia I went to school with him how did he know where to find me I thought he died over in Iraq.

King childhood friend Cisco had got recruited to the military as soon as they graduated from high school he was only gone a year, king thought the next time he saw Cisco outside his towers he would have some of his soldiers escort him in, king had heard some stories about Cisco being in Iraq he also heard he spent a little time in Afghanistan shooting at people who wasn't there the military psychiatrist said that Cisco was crazy as hell, so he got an early dismissal from the military, Cisco would write king talking out his head but king dismissed it thinking that his friend was coo coo for coco puffs, the last letter Cisco wrote king he was still living in Columbia he had no idea that king moved to Chicago until he made it back to Columbia from the military, when king left Columbia he had his address change to a post office box in Chicago, he knew all too well what was going on with Cisco because he used to write king all types of crazy shit at least once a week, even thou king knew for sure that Cisco was short of a six pack he would always be his dirty buddy know matter what.

One thing king learned from Cisco growing up was that the nigga was a real nigga when he said he was going to kill you he meant every word the nigga didn't take any shorts from anybody, Cisco was the type of hard core nigga that will split your head until the white meat show then turn around kick you in your ass and then put two in your head without even blinking his eyes, king wanted Cisco on his team but he had to find out first was he really missing in action in his head first, because he didn't have time for any errors, king knew before Cisco went into the service he was intelligent and vicious that's the way he remembered him and that's the way he's going to see him even thou he knows that Cisco may have a motive for coming to see him he had yet to find out why is he in the windy city.

King wasn't going to treat his friend dirty he was going to give him the benefit of doubt to see where his head really was and what were his intentions showing up in Chicago without even a invitation, king knew it was time for him to step up his security because there was no way in hell Cisco was suppose to be that close to king tower's without his foot soldiers not spotting an intruder friend or foe that shit wasn't going down in king towers, king knew he had to call a meeting immediately because his foot soldiers were getting sloppy and he had to put a handle on it real quick, king called Dallas to let him know that he wanted to go to the gun club to take his gal Aphrodite to teach her how to shot he wanted her to be able to handle herself when he wasn't around, the mysterious thing about Aphrodite she was scared shitless of guns and king knew it but that wasn't going to stop him from trying to teach her what she needed to know because time was of essences. king was going to see to it that Aphrodite had got a gun permit and she was going to learn how to shoot good enough to join the military snipers, when they arrived at the shooting range Aphrodite thought that king had lost his damn mine but she knew it had to be something seriously going down for her man to want her strapped, so she took king up on his offer and took the gun lessons, after they left the shooting range king dropped her back off at the crib and headed to king towers for the meeting he told all his soldiers that the meeting was mandatory no excuses, while king and his right hand men were pulling up in front of king towers he still felt uneasy because he felt like someone was still watching him, he was so deep in thought that he didn't even realize that they were in front of king towers he told himself he had to do some heavy investigation because he knew he was vicious as they come, but he knew it was some corruption going on in his camp and he had to find out who the culprit was a.s.a.p. he didn't know if he was being paranoid or was he just taking precautions but one thing he knew for sure he was going to settle this shit today.

King started the meeting with how his soldiers on the roof top were tripping ain't no nigga got no business hanging around my shit at all, if I want some stragglers hanging around I could go get some of them nigga's down off the corner, before king could say something else Bo—Pete told king it wasn't his fault I do my part it's them nigga's Juice and Bryce and them other nigga's fucking up not me, king told Bo—Pete to shut the fuck up because it ain't no I in team, king said now back to business before I was so rudely interrupted I want to add some more artillery to our fold, he pulled a box out from under the table ripped it open and there was eight 380's, ten Glock's, ten 50 cal's, Uzi's, m-16, and seven grenade launchers with AK—47, king meant when a nigga came at them he better be well strapped because if he didn't he was going to meet his maker for "sho".

The next thing king said was that he knew that he was being watch and it wasn't any coincident either king instinct was in high gear he knew something was out of character and it wasn't him just being paranoid either, whoever it was king was going to find out and he was going after their ass politically hood style he wasn't about to get caught slipping and he made it known to his soldiers, they had to remain alert at all times it wasn't no exceptions if he caught them slipping he was going to put two in their heads without a second thought and that was real talk, the next thing on the agenda was to check out speedy he was on king shit list he had a warning to be gone by sunrise and if he wasn't he wanted him hog tied and bought back to king for his demise, Dallas and Diego went on the set where speedy was hanging out but when they got there the police had all speedy crew sitting on the curve so Dallas and Diego sat there to see what was up, what they saw next blew them out of the water they seen the detectives take speedy out the car uncuff him and pat him on the back and told him he was free to go what puzzled Dallas and Diego the most was they hauled everybody else off to jail but this nigga got a free pass this meant one thing for sure this nigga speedy was a snitch.

Dallas couldn't wait to give king heads up on speedy he told king what went down and how the scene played out he also told king they were going to snatch his snitching ass up and take him to the warehouse, they wanted to kill speedy and chop his ass up but king told them to tie that muthafucka down until he gets there that's all they wanted to hear but it wasn't going to be a pretty picture when king showed up because it wasn't nothing that they hated more than a snitch, when king entered the warehouse he followed the blood splatter from the warehouse door, Dallas and Diego had beat speedy to a bloody pulp, he was screaming like a goat getting his nuts cut off for a fourth of July picnic, king looked in speedy eyes that were now swollen he said didn't I warn your punk ass what was gone happen if you didn't leave my city nigga, I don't make threats I make promises now I hear that you a muthafucking snitch too let's just chop this nigga up and feed his ass to the dogs.

Dallas and Diego was more than happy to oblige king with his request so they turned on the meat chopper and went to work on speed's ass, they put speedy in a meat grinder that was a chopper, that chopper was rotating speedy ass and grinding him as fine as cat hair the only thing left to do was bag his ass up for dog food, it wasn't until three days later when the detectives came looking for speedy when they notice that he haven't stayed in contact with them like he suppose to have done that's the only reason they were looking for him other than him being an informant for them speedy was just another drug dealer that no body gave a damn about period.

Now that the detectives thought speedy had bounced it was time for them to find another sucker to info trade king towers, even thou they knew deep down that speedy just didn't up and disappear it was evident that he might have got caught being a police informant because he was to weak for real, even thou he tried to play hard core in reality he was just a bitch in sheep clothing.

chapter eight

Gloria (Baby Girl) Bout It Bout It!

—•—

Baby girl was finding out more and more about Steven and the commissioner and also about his wifey and kids, he was still lying to her about his wife he said they had been separated for three years not knowing that baby girl knew more about his family life than he did, she even found out Steven had a chick on the side name Belinda that was more into Steven than she was, Belinda had pictures of baby girl and Steven on several dates, as baby girl was checking her out she was doing the same Steven has his hands full trying to jiggling three women he thought he had his shit together until Belinda busted his ass out, she was able to give Steven blow by blow of his outings with baby girl she also was able to tell Steven where baby girl stayed, he told Belinda that baby girl was only a business associate of his she told Steven you run that bull—shit to somebody else because I know for a fact nigga you been sleeping with that bitch, so you need to get your shit checked out because between me her and your wife one of us is going to be walking around with Chlamydia nigga and I promise you it isn't going to be me, you know what Steven if she is just your business associate like you said than why haven't I been introduced to her" huh"? Because you with your smart ass trying to have your cake and eat it too but you can pass me on that bull—shit because I'm done.

While Steven was at Belinda house trying to plead his case baby girl was sitting outside Belinda's house watching them interact with each other from Belinda's front bay window, she found out that Steven and Belinda had been dating for about two years she found out from one of the attorneys at Stevens firm that he was a heavy hitter when it came to the ladies, so baby girl dug up what she could to find out who Belinda Garcia was, when she saw that Belinda came from money and her mother was deceased and father was a medical physician she said to herself that Steven might be a ladies' man but the bastard had good taste, she hated to admit it but Belinda was gorgeous and she looked to be at least a year older than baby girl, baby girl thought that it was time to turn the tables a little bit on Steven so she decided to invite him to dinner along with his girlfriend Belinda, without Steven knowing that Belinda was her surprise guest for Steven she had plans to make a setting that he wouldn't forget, she had vanilla candles lit out threw her apartment he loved violet flowers she had the tables setup with violet flowers with white orchids added to them she had Luther soft music playing in the background she knew how slick men could be so just in case Steven told Belinda that they were just friends her plans would show and tell her differently.

Baby girl had her shit together she went shopping at the supermarket to pick up some crab legs, lobster, and shrimps with some wild rice with asparagus she even went in the wine department to make sure she had to bottles of Steven's favorite wine Cristal, she knew Belinda frequent that supermarket a lot so she made sure she would get things that Belinda loved to eat as well, she found out Belinda's face book page and became friends with her so when she found out Belinda was more interested in her than she should have been she invited her to her little surprise dinner party to see what really was going on with her and Steven without them knowing who was coming to her little dinner party for the three of them, baby girl decided tonight was going to be a beginning to an end for MR. Steven.

Steven arrived first he was smiling like he had just won award baby girl made sure she placed him in the kitchen while she put the dinner rolls in the oven, she was just about to tell Steven that her brother king was going to stop by and bring her something when the door bell started ringing, Steven got up and was getting ready to go to the door when baby girl stopped him, she said no sweetie I'll get the door I want you to sit there and relax, Steven never seen it coming because he was sitting with his back to the door talking to one of his partners at his law firm when Belinda stepped in the kitchen carrying another bottle of Cristal, when Steven looked up and seen Belinda it was like time had just stopped he went to stuttering trying to form sentences that couldn't come out he was choking off the Cristal he asked Belinda what are you doing here and how did you two meet? Belinda told Steven wouldn't you want to know I told your stupid ass what's done in the dark will soon come to light didn't I, Steven threw a fit he didn't know what to expect next he said y'all know what fuck you two bitches I don't have to deal with this shit y'all have the game twisted, before Steven left the situation got hot baby girl said I warned your ass what was going to happen if you kept playing with my emotions so here is my proposition, I need both of y'all to sit y'all ragged ass down when she up her 380and she said this is how this is going to play out either you can kill her Steven and walk out of my life as a free man our I can kill both you muthafuckas and call it a day now it's up to you player, Steven looked at Belinda with her Carmel

complexion with her hazel brown eyes and said it's nothing personal
sweetheart it's business it's either kill or be killed and I'm not putting
you before me so it's lights out baby I'm sorry.

Baby girl asked herself why would she fuck with Stevens selfish ass it
could have been the other way around what if it she was Belinda he
would of sold her ass out too to save his own ass, right after Steven
shot Belinda twice in the head he looked at baby girl and said the
stupidest shit, now what about us she said nigga is you stupid I can't
trust your lying ass it's a wrap nigga I might as well put a fork in your
ass because your done.

Right when Steven thought he was going to wrap things up with baby
girl she had planned the element of surprise for Steven, she really had
turned the table completely around on Steven she had mapped out
Stevens demise with his wife she flew in from Atlanta so she could be
in on the plan to, she wasn't surprise that Steven was cheating on her
because she had caught him before plus he was on strike three and
this time it was going to cost Steven his life, once Steven seen Jennie
come out of baby girl's bedroom he knew it was truly over for him
that ass started begging like Keith Sweat at one of his concerts, Jennie
wasn't hearing his sad ass stories she grabbed her 38 out of her purse
and shot Steven three times in the chest at point blank range she
dropped Steven so fast that he didn't even get a chance to plead his
case his eyes was wide open staring Jennie right in the eyes.

Baby girl called the cleaners to come get the two dead bodies out of
her apartment she didn't want her son smoke to come in and see dead
bodies laying in a pool of blood on her floor, plus she didn't want

her son to know yet that she was an assassin in reality she didn't want him to see that side of her at all she want smoke to see nothing but the best side of his mother, once the cleaners arrived at baby girl's apartment she was more than happy to let them in she wanted them gone before her son came home from school, Jennie on the other hand had to come up with a reason to tell her son's why their father wasn't never coming home, after the cleaners cleaned up baby girl's apartment and left she gave Jennie a ride back to the airport they made an agreement to never mention Steven again baby girl also had Jennie's address just in case she tried to cross her so she would know where to find her she already knew where Jennie's family stayed she even knew where Jennie worked so it wasn't going to be a problem locating her if she needed her.

chapter nine

Cane (Smoke) Chaning Lanes

---•●•---

Cane (smoke) baby girl son started feeling like his mother was up to some shady shit so he decided it was time he started to do his own investigating, he felt like her and king was up to a lot of corruption and he wanted to know what it was and if it meant him missing some more days out of school to find out what the hell was going on than so be it, what smoke little young ass was about to find out was going to fuck his young mind up he had followed his mother to her office, he had snuck into the backseat of her car and covered his self up with a blanket that she kept on her back seat.

Once baby girl pulled into the parking lot of her office she retrieved her brief case off the seat and got out of her car and went into the building, once she got in the building and went into her office she didn't think to look back at her car to see that her back door to her car was a jarred, smoke had slid out the back door of the car and was on his way to sneak into his mothers law firm through the back door, he knew something wasn't right with his mother and his uncle king and he wanted to know what the two of them were hiding from him, when smoke went in through the back door baby girl and her friends were so caught up in their conversation that they didn't notice that the silent alarm had went off until they received a call from the police dispatch asking them if they needed assistance, smoke went into his mothers office and hid in her coat closet while she was out in the lobby talking with Ava and Denise about the handsome twin brothers they met name Kaylen and Keith.

When baby girl got the call from the police she decided she would check her perimeters to make sure that it wasn't anyone in her place of business that wasn't supposed to be there, once her and her girls got through giving their office a once over they started their conversation back up again talking about the bitches they hired for kings trafficking, they went on to talk about how smoke had been fucking up at school lately, baby girl told Ava and Denise that if she hadn't been raped by them crazy ass men Jose and his crazy ass henchmen she wouldn't have ever gotten pregnant, when smoke heard his mother say she had been raped and he was the product of what came out of the rape he was angry and hurt he didn't know how to except what he had just heard, so smoke just stayed in that hot ass closet until he was able to come out and that wasn't until baby girl and her friends left the office going to lunch.

When smoke did make it out of his mother's closet at her law firm he felt like someone hit him in his heart with a bow and arrow, he had only made it a couple blocks away before he broke down he couldn't believe that his father and maybe his friends could be his father due to the rape they committed on his mother, smoke couldn't think straight he was very confused and hurt because he had been asking his mother for years about his father but she would always play him to the left, she nevered seem to want to talk about who he was and why every time he would mention father or dad in the same sentence would make his mother mad enough to walk out the house and slammed the door, now that smoke knew the details of why his mother never

57

talked to him about his old dude, now he knew, smoke wanted to kill Jose and his friends for what they did to his mother but he's was a little too late his father had been wiped off the face of the earth before he was even born.

Cane (smoke) was so overwhelmed with what he heard his mother say about his father that he went in front of a liquor store waiting on someone to go in, so he could pay them to bring him a bottle of Seagram's Gin out of the store so he could try to drink his sorrows away, it was a woman that was getting ready to enter the liquor store when smoke asked her if she wanted to make twenty dollars the woman looked like she had been drinking alcohol all her life but she looked at smoke she said what you want me to do for you for twenty dollars? because if I give you a blow job it's going to cost your young ass fifty dollars, smoke looked at the nasty lady that was standing in front of him and said look lady I don't want your trifling ass doing shit to me personally, all I want you to do is go in the store and buy me a bottle of Gin that's it after that you can go on about your business "Aight", the lady told smoke give me the money with your smart mouth ass I'll do it this time but don't you ever speak to a lady like that again smoke waited until she came out the store with his Gin before he told her what he really wanted to say, you're not a fucking lady you're a crack head but I'll respect what you said I won't disrespect you again because I won't be back in this hood again so thanks for my bottle and have a good day.

Smoke turned around and headed back on his side of town he knew his mother wouldn't be home so he arrived home went down in the basement pop the top on his bottle of Gin and started drinking,

smoke was sitting down in his basement drinking and talking to
himself about how his family was keeping secrets from him, and
his father is a rapist and his grandmother disappeared for two years
without a trace of her whereabouts and know ones tells him anything,
the only thing he's ever told is go to school get a education and do
good things with your life, while all the time they doing shit that's
off the fucking chain, by the time he had finished his bottle of Gin
he was in rear form he had build up his courage to kick some shit off
with his mother and his uncle king, he wanted to call them out on
this so—called drug empire that they had established everybody knew
what was going down and who was running shit but him, but it was
time to settle this shit for real because he was about to be fifteen he
was a big boy not a kid and they wasn't going to keep hiding things
from him it was going to be laid out on the table today he wants to
be a part of the family business.

Smoke was so upset about what he heard his mother say it just kept
playing over and over in his head like a broken record, he wanted to
ask his mother why did she keep a child that was the product of a
rapist, he wasn't in any shape to talk to his mother or his uncle king
because he was drunk for one, and second he wasn't ready for the
shit that his mother had to drop on him, it wasn't his time yet but
when baby girl made it home and heard a loud sound coming from
the basement she grabbed her gun from her purse because Smoke
was supposed to be at school not in her basement drinking gin, when
she finally reached the bottom of the basement steps she seen her
son sitting in the corner on the floor with a empty Gin bottle with
his head down low saying to himself that he was in a dysfunctional
family were everyone was keeping secret from him.

Baby girl was so caught up in doing her own thing until she forgot that smoke needed her guidance he wasn't a client of hers he was her son, that's why smoke never paid attention to what his mother had to say it would go on deaf ears he found it hard to pay attention to someone that never paid attention to him unless he was doing something wrong, he felt that his mother paid more attention to her brother and her law firm than him, he just thought that if he started drinking all his pain would subside just for a little while, when baby girl took the bottle out of her sons hand she asked him what was his problem? Smoke told his mother why you want to know you don't give a flying shit about me you only acknowledge me when I get in trouble, since you want to know what's wrong mother dear I can tell you why the hell didn't you tell me my father and his friends beat and raped you and why has my grandmother left me with you and you can't see past your ass to know I even exist, I want to know what the hell is going on in this family and I want to know now! Or I'm going to bounce and you would never see me again and that's a promise, baby girl didn't know her son had built up so much animosity toward her it wasn't that he hated his mother he just wanted her to show him the loved that she showed everyone else, baby girl grabbed her son and started hugging him to let him know she loved him with all her heart when she realized that his body had went limp, she started screaming somebody help me when all of a sudden smoke opened his eyes to look at her and what baby girl seen next scared the shit out of her, it wasn't smoke anymore Jose had posted up inside of smokes body to let baby girl know about what he told her one night when he came to visit her in Columbia when she gave birth to their son he looked at her with those green eyes he said I told you he was going to be just like me, meaning that Jose was being reborn right then and there in smokes body as he was laying in his mother's arms on the floor drunk as hell, he could only take over smokes body when he just gave up living right when smoke thought that he couldn't live with the lies and disappointment of his mother he just stopped breathing and his father Jose rapist ass slid right in to destroy baby girl and kings empire.

But little did Jose know taking over smoke body for a while will be short lived because smoke was tougher than his dead ass daddy Jose gave him credit for,

Smoke didn't know his father was an earth bound spirit and so was his grandfather Cane the one he gotten his name from and he was taking back what belong to the Carters and that was smoke he wasn't about to let Jose take his granddaughters only child without a fight the devil worked in mysterious ways and he was working the shit out of Jose and his friends they kept the devils pick fork full of flame burning in their backs, baby girl knew her son was having an out of body experience when he gave her the same funny grin the night she met Jose she wanted him to move on and leave her and her son alone, smoke was changing lanes quick going back and forward she told smoke baby you can fight him you are stronger than him he's a week man by himself, the next thing she saw was smoke eyes changing back to their normal color and he was reaping of gin he started vomiting like crazy he had no idea of what had just happen to him but he was feeling very strange.

———————————— •●• ————————————

chapter ten

Kaylen And Keith Calling For Reinforcements

Keith and Kaylen had been watching king every move they knew
that he didn't travel the same circles every day he didn't even drive in
the same vehicle, they even watched how king handled his soldiers
they knew in order to go full force up against king they had to call in
some well owed favors from guys that will kill a nigga just on general
principle, Keith told Kaylen we need to handle this shit and quick
so I'm going to call a couple of favors in to Mad Max and the rest of
his crew, Dante known as the (shovel) Steve known's as the (tooth
pick killer) mad dog Lester known as (baby face) and black who go
by (charcoal) when Keith called them they was more than happy to
help in their mast of destruction because a great deal of money was
involved in killing this nigga they knew as king.

Kaylen told his brother that they had to go check this nigga out name
money because he had some shit with some fire power that will bring
kings army of soldiers to their knees, Keith said for real let's go pay
this nigga a visit then, kaylen called money and he told them to bring
plenty of cash because as soon as he sold them what they wanted
in fire arms he was going to bounce because he didn't want king
coming after him next, when the twins made it over to money's they
watched as money pulled open a sliding door that had nothing but
m249-machine guns, spring mp5 machine guns, mga3 pkm-t180,
ultimax 106 mk-2 machine guns, pp-90m machine guns, fmg9

folding machine guns, with 2 elephant guns so they were gearing up for the war but were they going to survive the war was the question, money charged Keith and Kaylen a grip for his fire arms they wasn't mad that they had to spend fifty thousand dollars in fire arms because they knew it was going to be worth every dime, mean while they thought that they should go back and put some more sex down on Ava and Denise to modify their behavior so that they could get some information on king and his soldiers, kaylen told Keith nigga you tripping because if you put that shit downright she will be following behind your ass like a wet puppy, before Keith could say anything else they both fell out laughing real hard because he knew that they couldn't keep up with Ava and Denise because they had both of the twins pussy whipped.

Kaylen said nigga I have never prayed in my life but this time we need to pray that we make it out this shit alive for real, Keith said what's the problem nigga you scared if you are you need to take your black ass to church nigga because what we about to do don't have shit to do with god this the devils work fool, now come on with all that" sucka" shit let's pack our shit in the mustang and move on out, kaylen told his brother that he was talking some stupid shit because stupidity overrides ignorance every time, this shit needs our undivided attention because in this game every man for his damn self there's no rules your weakest link can easily be replace as long as you rule with a iron fist, you can write that shit in blood nigga and take it to the bank for real, you just have to learn to listen nigga, in order to make our way to the top we have to take the nigga at the top down and king is that nigga so stop thinking about pussy and dying all the time and think about the job at hand.

63

Keith didn't like the fact that his brother was talking to him like he was crazy but he knew one thing for sure that he was right about what he was saying he just didn't want to tell him that, he knew that greed and envy appreciate distinguish and probably ignored a lot in the drug world, the twins was so overwhelmed with killing king they started smoking weed purple haze was Keith's favorite he would get a buzz and think he was invincible, Kaylen would stay in his ass a lot about letting his guards down Keith said look here I know what the hell I'm doing stop getting hostile with me nigga I got this you need to chill the fuck out my brother, you going to mess around and give yourself a damn concussion tripping off of what I'm doing, the phone ringing in Keith pocket stop them from arguing with each other it was mad Max letting them know that they were about to touch down in two hours and where they could meet up at.

Mad Max had all ready rented him and his crew three rooms at a sleazy hotel on the out skirts of Chicago so that when they made their introduction's to king and his soldiers they could bounce, Mad Max had a freak name Patricia that stayed in Chicago that he used hit whenever he was in the windy city so he thought that he will call her for some much need sex while he was in town, once he called Patricia and got conformation from her that she would meet him at the stop n go hotel his adrenaline was pumping because she could be worse than a beast with two backs and he loved every minute of it, he was getting a convulsion just thinking about it so he stopped to focus on the situation at hand it was killing this nigga king so they all could get rich.

While Kaylen and Keith were waiting on Mad Max and his crew to pull up they were sitting in front of king towers strapped with their glock 380, they had been there since they left moneys house they even purchased high powered binoculars so they could have a close view on what was going on around king towers perimeters, the brothers knew king had his shit locked down but to see a nigga younger than them doing the damn thing was upsetting to them because they wasn't born with a silver spoon in their mouth, they had to do what it took to survive and it wasn't easy trying to come up to where they are now, being hired guns is not what they had in mind but it keeps the bills paid and it keeps them with shit they never had before, while they were sitting there watching king Keith phone started ringing again this time it was tooth pick letting them know that they would be pulling into the hotel in twenty minutes and for them to be there, so he told Kaylen nigga we need to bounce our nigga's should be at the hotel by the time we get there Kaylen said "Aight" let's roll on out then we can come back for this nigga after we regroup.

Keith thought once he ran shit down to everybody about king operations that they would wait until it got dark to check his ass, but Mad Max had other plans he wanted to peep shit out first to see what they were up against before they struck, so he told the brothers that once it got dark they were going to camp outside king towers to see what this nigga handle is and then and only then will they come up with a plan to take him down, Mad Max told them he didn't come all the way from Michigan for no bull—shit he came to stick and move.

Keith knew he called a furious group of crazy ass nigga when he made that call to Mad Max everyone of them had spent time in jail from armed robbery to drug trafficking to murder so it wasn't going to be a problem trying to keep them in line, when the twins made it to the hotel where Mad max and the crew were staying Kaylen couldn't get the thought out of his mine that they made a mistake about calling in Mad Max and his crew, he had strong vibes about how Mad Max wants to control what him and his brother is there to do and he wasn't having it, but he did listen to what their plans were to take king down off his throne, after Mad Max told the brothers that he was going to be the one running the whole show the shit hit the fan because Keith was the one put in the called to them in the first place knowing that Mad Max and his crew owed favors to them he was just calling in favors not for them to come to Chicago to take over what him and his brother had plan.

Kaylen told Keith this nigga tripping if he thinks he's going to come here and run shit we invested our time and money in artillery for this take down of king, what the twins didn't know was Mad Max shiesty ass was up to know good he had already inform his men once they take out king and his foot soldiers they were going to take Kaylen and Keith out as well, but they dumb as didn't give the twins credit because Kaylen peeped game early in the conversation he knew it was some shit in the game, once the meeting was over and the twins left the hotel and got back in their car and pulled off Keith asked Kaylen did he hear that shit Mad Max was talking, he said sure I heard that lame ass shit but that nigga is going to be sleeping with the fish's as soon as we take down king his ass and his men is going to be a wrap. The next day the twin were suppose to meet up with Mad Max and his crew to take them to show them were king towers was, but what they didn't know was the twins had thought long and hard about switching sides because in reality they knew they didn't stand a chance against king and his foot soldiers, they thought if they got in more with Ava and Denise they might have a chance of come out of this situation a live, the twins still haven't noticed they had a shadow in the background Jasper Buddha's brother was still keeping a close eye on them he was watching them when they went to the hotel to meet up with Mad Max and his crew, he liked their style because he knew one thing for sure that they defiantly was going to need back up going up against king because he had been watching king also and he knew the power that the young kid carried, Kaylen really didn't want to chance being involved with Mad Max and his crew he knew that they were trying to come up with a takeover and he was going to see to it him and his brother came out on top.

Mean while when the twins was having breakfast and a meeting with Mad Max and his crew in walks king and his right hand men and foot soldiers, they were all having breakfast at the international house of pancakes when Mad Max looked up and said who is that little nigga with all them nigga's following behind him like he own the world, Keith said nigga that's your target king, Mad max said come on my nigga you mean to tell me that young nigga running the windy city, yeah homie that's him in the flesh, alright now that we know who we looking for it's about to go down in the windy city, Mad Max couldn't stop staring at king because he couldn't believe a young nigga like king had Chicago on lock like he had been hearing.

Kaylen told Keith I don't trust that nigga he just like a penny two faced and worthless all Keith could say was no doubt, Keith told his brother we are going to stay as close to that nigga as the drawers he's wearing because it's some shit about to jump off and I will be damn if we get caught up in the cross fire, but right now we are going to treat this nigga with kindness because kindness is the biggest gun you can shoot as long as your aim is on point, Kaylen responded with a true that, king sat down at the table three rows from the twins and Mad Max and his crew but he kept getting a feeling that someone was mugging him so when he looked up he was eye to eye with Mad Max they held on to their stares for all of two minutes until king asked was there a problem before Mad Max could answer Detroit went up to their table to get a good look at this want to be tough ass nigga, Mad Max didn't like the idea that Detroit approached his table and tried to punk him in front of his crew, he told Detroit look I'm new in town and I was just checking out my surroundings that's all is that a crime these days? Detroit told Mad Max it is if you staring at a nigga like you want to start something it is partner.

Kaylen and Keith really was at the wrong place at the wrong time because they really didn't want to be caught with Mad Max and his crew knowing what they were in town to do, Mad Max was going on the south side of Chicago to meet up with his little freak Patricia she had been blowing his phone up since he arrived in Chicago just thinking about getting his head waxed was making his dick jump in his pants, once breakfast was over everybody decided to meet back up at the hotel for one on one stalking of kings towers, what the twins didn't know at the time was that Jasper was sitting in the back of the restaurant watching the whole scene unfold right before his eyes he knew then that Mad Max and his crew was going to be more trouble than they were worth, Jasper said to himself I don't think these fools value common sense because they're not using it wisely they already been peeped out by their target he knows how each and every one of them look now how stupid can they be. When Mad Max made it to Patricia's house he got out his car and knock on her door she opened the door stock butt naked she was glowing with her body running water from her jumping out the shower without drying off her body, Mad Max looked at her and started licking his lips because he was going to get freaked down from head to toe, what made Mad Max didn't know was the last time he was with Patricia two years ago she had gotten pregnant by him and never told him she didn't want him to ever find out they had a son together because he made sure he let her know he didn't want in kids so he would always strap up but she took his rubber and put pin holes in it so she would carry his seed without him knowing what she did.

While Mad Max was over there getting his freak on his crew was sitting outside kings towers stalking king, it was crazy that day because they were stalking king and Jasper was stalking them and king's undercover cops was stalking all of them and reporting back to king about all the stalking activity that was taking place outside his perimeter, king decide that if its war that they want let's let the cards fall where they lay that way they can get what they came to king towers to get killed.

Keith and Kaylen decided why be ignorant they knew for sure they had some high powered artillery but they didn't have the man power to go up against king and his army of soldiers, so they decided to jump ship quick they waned Ava and Denise to set them up with a meeting with king so they could let him know what was going on, when Keith called Ava to explain to her why he hadn't been spending that much time with her she really didn't want to hear it until he told her the truth about why him and Kaylen were really in Chicago, after Keith told her the truth the phone went silent he thought she had hung up but she didn't she knew when they met it was too good to be true, it just seem like every time her and Denise would go out for lunch they would pick up bad guys she thought that they were just cursed with a bad omen.

Ava called Denise and baby girl to run down the scenario that Keith had just gave her to see what they had to say about it, when they heard what Ava had to say baby girl was ready to murder both of the brothers for being stupid enough to announce that they were paid to kill her brother, but Denise on the other hand was glad they came clean because she really did care for Kaylen a lot and to see him buried six feet deep would have been heartfelt for her to stomach, one thing that concern Denise was that they all had ugliness in them and for them to judge Kaylen and Keith for admitting that they were there to bring king down wouldn't be right at least they found out early that they wasn't going to win that battle.

Baby girl decided that she will give them a pass this time but she can't say the same for her brother he might have a different attitude than she does, baby girl set the meeting up with king and the twins to see what was up but she was most definitely going to be there because if something kicked off she was going to make sure that the twins would regret ever crossing paths with angel carters children.

———————————•●•———————————

chapter eleven

Jasper Taking Control

———•·—

Jasper was still tailing Kayen and Keith when he pulled into a parking space two rows behind them at club sexy he didn't have a chance to get out the car when he seen king and his entourage pull up and get out and go into the club, right when Jasper made his mine up to go inside baby girl and her crew pulled in behind him so he was pretty much ready to go in because in his mine something shady was going down and he wanted to know exactly what was going on, once everybody got inside the club Jasper made his exit from his car and went inside the club he slid into a booth in the corner so he could have a good view, when he seen Kaylen and Keith walk in and sit at the same table that king and his crew was sitting at he knew then that the tables had turned, Jasper said to himself I can't believe these two nigga's betrayed me but it's cool it's all gravy because I'm going to kill them two snitching ass nigga's I should of known better to hire nigga's I don't know for real, that's alright because I have something for their assess when they get back to their hotel, Jasper sat there a little longer to see what was coming next when he seen king get up and draw his gun in the direction of the two brother 's he was so angry that he was spitting every time he said something, so Jasper thought that if king keep up his charade he might not have to kill the two brothers king would of done him a favor in taking the two of them out.

King was pissed because he had all these soldiers around him and know body noticed shit so he had to tighten down on his soldiers, all while Jasper was sitting back in the cut watching them king's undercover cops was watching Jasper they couldn't believe how much he looked like Buddha they knew they killed him but seeing Jasper was like déjà vu, it made the two cops second guess their selves so they decided to keep a close eye on Jasper to make sure it wasn't a bad dream they were having and to see what made Buddha's look alike come to Chicago to spy on king, they knew everybody thought that king killed Buddha only they knew the truth they thought but king had a surprise for their assess to he knew that the two dirty cops set him up it was just a matter of time before he hung their assess out to dry.

King didn't want to except Keith and Kaylen's proposal until he was sure they were loyal to their word so to make sure their word was bond he gave them a ultimatum he wanted them to kill his two dirty cops, and to make sure that they carried out his order he wanted Detroit and Dallas to go along with them because if they didn't kill them king gave orders for Dallas and Diego to kill Kaylen and Keith.

Jasper left the club and went to sit in his car to wait on Kaylen and Keith he was so deep in thought that he didn't notice his back door to his car was being open by the two dirty cops that had been watching him since the day he came to Chicago watching king towers, once Johnson and Williamson got in the backseat of Jasper car he wasn't surprised at all he told them I know you two crooked ass cops work for king I also know that you been watching me just like I been watching you, now that we been formally introduced what the fuck do y'all want? Johnson said don't worry about what we want you need to be worry about what's going to happen to your ass once we tell king that Buddha's brother is in town stalking him and trying to kill him.

Jasper told Johnson and Williamson I couldn't give a flying shit what you two ass holes tell him because right now the way things look you two bastards is out of control and one phone call and you two will be dead before sunrise, Johnson said you threatening us you piece of shit, Jasper told them I don't make threats I make promise's, Williamson was so angry that he grabbed Jasper from behind and put his thirty eight up to his temple he said now I'm going to say this only once if you don't get the hell out of Chicago by tomorrow morning you going to be found dead just like your brother Buddha was with your stomach cut wide the hell open, what Williamson didn't realize is that his dumb ass just admitted to Jasper that him and his partner killed his brother not king, Jasper told them that he was leaving Chicago first thing in the morning but in the back of his mine he wasn't leaving into he put them two dirt mother fuckers in the ground for the death of his brother Buddha.

Jasper thought it was time for him to take control all this time he been looking at the situation in the wrong way, yes king was responsible for the murder of his son but not his brother and before he left town he was going to see to that they be held responsible for what they did to his family, one thing Jasper learned over the years was that family is like baking a cake from scratch it's real messy but it's still your family, Jasper went back to his room at the hotel and packed his bags because he wasn't going to be staying there any longer he was going to be living out his car for a few days until he came up with a plan to take Johnson and Williamson out first, he switched up from stalking king to stalking the two dirty cops Johnson and Williamson he even switched cars he rented a dark blue minivan so he wouldn't so suspicious, he followed Williamson home first and found out he was married with two children he made plans to wait outside until he left home, Jasper was outside Williamson house for an hour and a half before he came out to leave once he did Jasper seen his wife walk him out to his car screaming obscenities at him, which would be in Jaspers favor because it was a neighbor coming home from the store that seen everything that transpired between the two of them.

Jasper had planned on killing Williamson's family he got out of his car and walked around the neighborhood to make sure he didn't see anyone so he couldn't get recognized by anyone, he had chloroform in his pocket to put them to sleep with he wasn't as hard core as his brother Buddha was especially when it came to killing children but this time it was different because Jasper was out for revenge against the people who tore his family apart, Jasper went up to Williamson back door and broke out the back window Mrs. Williamson didn't hear a thing because she was upstairs in the bedroom.

Jasper crept up the stairs to find Mrs. Williamson in the bathroom she was just getting out of the shower with her back turned to Jasper when he snuck up behind her and put the chloroform rag up to her nose, she tried to fight him off of her when all a sudden her body went limp when Jasper picked her up and laid her across the bed, once Jasper made sure she was knocked out from the chloroform he went into the children's bedroom to see if they were still asleep but the children were nowhere to be found they were at their grandmothers house for the weekend that's something that Jasper didn't count on, Jasper made it back into the bedroom and Mrs. Williamson was still stretch out across the bed Jasper had a butcher knife that he retrieved from the kitchen, he went back in the bedroom and stuck the knife into Mrs. Williamson stomach the same way that Mr. Williamson the dirty cop did to his brother Buddha when he killed him, he even went as far as carving Buddha's name into her forehead letting detective Williamson know that pay back is a bitch and then you die.

Before Jasper left the Williamson house he washed down everything he touched while he was inside their house he even took the butcher knife with him because he was planning on using that same knife to kill Williamson and Johnson with it, Jasper went to where he knew that the two dirty cops would be sitting so he would be watching after he made the call to the police about the killing of Mrs. Williamson when they pulled off to go to detectives Williamson house he would be there sitting down the street so he could see him break down the same way he did when his son and brother were murdered, right after Jasper put the call in it went over the police radio loud and clear when Johnson and Williamson heard the address they speed off down the street because Williamson knew it was his house that they just put across the radio but he wasn't expecting what he saw once he got there his wife was laying across the bed split open the same way he did Buddha he knew then who was responsible for her death and with Buddha's name across her forehead was a sign that he would remember the rest of his life.

Jasper was sitting down the street watching the scene unfold he even
seen the morgue van when it pulled up to take Mrs. Williamson body
out in a black bag, he couldn't wait to see when detective Williamson
came and broke down in front of all his fellow officers he said to
himself yeah cry now because tomorrow your dirty ass will be in the
morgue with your wife with a tag on your toe, the police evidence
truck stayed at detective Williamson house for hours they couldn't
find any evidence of foul play until they went into the kitchen and
found the back door window broken out but it wasn't any finger
prints any where Jasper made sure of that, one of the detectives from
homicide felt that it was something very strange about the murder
of Mrs. Williamson because why would someone carve Buddha on
her forehead if it wasn't meant for detective Williamson to know who
this person was, to detective Donald this was a warning to detective
Williamson and he knew very well who this person was.

Jasper said one down and two more to go he wasn't going to be as
nice to detective Williamson and Johnson he was going to make them
bleed very slow and painful, Johnson pulled Williamson to the side he
said you know as well as I do that Buddha's brother did this you know
you let it slip that we killed his brother when we had him hemmed
up in his car the other day remember, Williamson said I'm killed that
bastard with my bare hands as soon as we catch up with him, but first
the captain wants' me to come in for questioning because they have
a wittiness that seen me auguring with my wife before I left home
today, we were auguring because I haven't been spending that much
time with my family lately and she had made dinner plans with her
family for Sunday dinner and I told her I wasn't going to be able to
make it because I had to work, the last word I'm going to remember

from my wife is fuck off was the last word she spoke to me before I pulled out of my driveway.

Jasper had his mine made up he was tired of playing cat and mouse games with the two detectives he had purchased some C4 from this guy he knew in from Jamaica, he was going to wire it up to their vehicle and watch it explode but first he had to wait for them to be out of it long enough to tape the C4 under Neath the vehicle first, to Jasper surprise the two detectives went into the station to talk with their captain and while they were out of the car Jasper put the C4 right up under the vehicle right in front of the police station, he set the timer that he had to the C4 to go off in two hours that would give them time to talk with their captain and come back out the station and go park outside of kings tower again like they do every day.

All Jasper could think about was if they go back and sit outside king towers maybe he could kill two birds with one stone he could blow up king's tower also, Jasper was sitting in his van outside the police station for an half an hour before the detectives came out got into their car and headed back to kings tower like he thought, but what he couldn't get out of his head was why was detective Williamson out on the street and not held accountable for his wife's murder, Jasper wasn't paying attention while he was in detective Williamson house the whole time he was looking all over the house and wiping down evidence and killing Mrs. Williamson he was being recorded the Williamson's had mini camera's all over their house he was the star in every camera, the only place he didn't come into view was the Williamson bathroom that's why Williamson and Johnson went into the station the commissioner was putting an all point bulletin out for Jasper and he didn't have a clue that he was captured on camera killing Mrs. Williamson.

While Jasper was on his way back to see the twins Kaylen and Keith at their hotel room he got spotted by one of the police cruisers when he didn't stop at a stop sign he was so into thought that he really didn't pay attention to the stop sign and rolled straight threw it, he didn't notice what he had done until the police put the sirens on and pulled him over, one of the officers asked him for his licenses and insurance card once he noticed that Jasper was from Jamaica he wanted to know what brought him to the windy city of Chicago, Jasper felt compelled not to answer that question because he wasn't about to tell the officers he was there to make sure that his hired guns killed king.

The officers told Jasper to stay put until they ran his driver's license, Jasper knew something wasn't right because they were taking too long to return back to his car with the ticket he thought he was going to get, but in reality they wasn't going to give Jasper a ticket he was going to be hauled off to jail for the murder of Mrs. Williamson, Jasper watched the two officers threw his rearview mirror and they were also staring back at him when he notice two more police cruisers pull up he knew they were up to something and he wasn't going quietly, Jasper pulled his 9mm from under his seat and put it beside his right leg when the other two officers got out of their car and started walking toward Jasper's car he speed off down the street, they jump in their car and speed off down the street behind Jasper in a police chase they were driving so fast trying to capture Jasper until Jasper made a quick right turn into a supermarket parking lot almost hitting a pregnant woman, Jasper hit the lady's shopping cart knocking it up in the air it came down right on top of one of the police cruisers causing the police cruiser to hit two more parked cars on the supermarket parking lot, the police cruiser hit the cars so hard it blew up the police cruisers transmission, the other two officers that was chasing Jasper called on the radio for more backup and for an ambulance for the other two officers that had the accident while they continue with the pursuit in chasing Jasper.

Jasper didn't have a clue to where he was going he was just trying to escape the police chase, Jasper turned down a dead end alley where he was trapped, it was a empty ran down building to his left all the windows were busted out of the building, Jasper jumped out his car and clamed in one of the windows he ran up some stairs that lead to the roof where he jumped across to the connecting roof and went down some more stairs leading to a crack house it was cracked out people everywhere he grabbed a man and asked him if he helped him find a way out of the building that he would give him fifty dollars the man was more than happy to help Jasper because that was more money for him to continue getting high with.

The man known as sonny lead Jasper down in the basement of the crack house where it was a side door that lead to a bar right off the alley, Jasper was able to sit inside the bar for a little while until the police officers did a door to door search, it was this woman in the bar who was watching Jasper when he came in the door sweating she was the bartender in the bar, she seen fear in Jasper eye's and decided that she could help him and maybe he could help her to out of a bad situation that she was in with her abusive boyfriend Floyd, she had a beat-up old Chevy out back that she could hide him in her trunk until the smoke clears for now, Jasper excepted the lady's idea because he wasn't trying to get caught by the law so far away from home, he asked the lady I'm sorry for getting you involve in my problems by the way what is your name? She said people around here call me sugar and we can talk later after the police get through with their searches if you don't mind.

Jasper stayed in sugars trunk for hours he even fell asleep it's a good thing sugar had bullet holes in her trunk because Jasper would have died if her car wasn't getting any air through the bullet holes she had in old Bessie, the name old Bessie came from the car being so old she would say old Bessie every time she would try to start it up the car would back fire and black smoke would come out of the tail pipe.

Jasper got the help he needed to escape the police with sugar's help she got off work at seven and drove home before she opened up her trunk to let Jasper out, he was so thankful to sugar for helping him he asked sugar was there anything he could do for her and she smiled and said as a matter of fact I do, sugar told Jasper the story of her abusive boyfriend and how he used to beat her for breakfast, lunch and dinner and sometimes snacks, he couldn't believe that a woman as sweet as sugar could be caught up with some man that didn't appreciate her, he told sugar that he would handle Floyd for her and for her not to worry because it would be a dark day before he put his hands on her again.

Right when sugar was about to give Jasper the information on Floyd he came stumbling thru the door drunk and calling sugar's name, he said sugar get your trifling ass out here I know you are here I see that piece of shit car of yours in the driveway, when Floyd turn down the hallway to sugars kitchen he was met with a cast Iron skillet across the head by Jasper he didn't even see it coming Jasper knocked Floyd out cold and put him a chair and tied him up, Jasper wanted sugar to torcher Floyd the way he had did her for the past five years of their relationship, sugar didn't really want to make him suffer like she did she wanted Floyd dead he had beat sugar and rape her in way's you couldn't imagine, she still had nightmares of what he did to her every time she looked him in his face and to sugar the only way to get rid of the nightmares was to get rid of Floyd, sugar looked at Jasper with desperation in her eyes she told Jasper to hand her the cast Iron skillet, she took that skillet and beat Floyd until he just slumped over in the chair everything he done to sugar came out of her every time she would swing that skillet at Floyd, she would say I hate you over and over until Jasper grabbed the skillet from sugar but it was too late Floyd was dead and sugar and Jasper became friends like the doll chucky would say we are friends to the end.

———————————— •❧• ————————————

chapter tweleve

Baby Girl Being Equally Yoked!

———————————•◦•———————————

Gloria (baby girl) decided she was done with Steven she wasn't going to become second or third in his womanizing behavior she was either going to be number one or she wasn't going to be in his life period so she called Steven to have a meeting with him about their so—call relationship, Steven was glad that baby girl called him they haven't spoken to each other in weeks since she found out that Steven not only was married with children but he also had a girlfriend on the side, baby girl knew it was time to let Steven move on with his life because that's exactly what she was about to do, she was really trying to convince herself that he would be better off dealing with his wife and his girlfriend before her and that she didn't have time to be playing games with a married man.

When baby girl finished up her phone call with Steven she was sitting at her desk looking at some file's when she heard her door open to her office when she looked up it was this dark skinned six feet tall chocolate brother walk in her office with Ava and Denise close on his trail, his dark skin was smooth as a babies bottom and he had tattoos over at least eighty percent of his body, he was smelling good enough to eat he was wearing baby girls favorite men's cologne Kenneth Cole Black, all baby girl could think about was who was this specimen of a man who stood before her and what he could possible want with her services, the young man reached his hand out to baby girl to introduce himself as Rashad peoples a.k.a. Brooklyn he had heard about baby girl through a mutual friend, he did his research on her as well he knew she was a kick ass attorney and who would be better to represent him then the woman he had been lusting for, Rashad asked Gloria a.k.a. Baby girl if he could take her to lunch so that they could talk in private about his case she accepted and they left her office for a more private location without her nosey associate's ear hustling in on their conversation.

Baby girl knew she was going to have to give Ava and Denise the information that Rashad was going to give to her because they wasn't going to rest until they found out what exactly this handsome man wanted and what kind of trouble that he was in that he wanted them to represent him, Rashad told baby girl that he had been in hiding for two years and that he was wanted for first degree murder, and that he was tired of running he wanted to feel free to walk around like everyone else did, baby girl asked Rashad what happen to make him commit murder? He told her that he came home from work late one evening and he could hear his mother screaming from her bedroom he also said he could hear things being thrown around the room, he said when he broke the door down to his mothers bedroom her boyfriend was standing over his mother beating her with a clothes hanger he was hitting her so hard until the hanger was literally cutting into her skin with every swing of the clothes hanger, his mother was balled up on the floor holding her hands over her face while this man beat blood out of her with a clothes hanger, Rashad told baby girl he lost it he jumped on top of his mother's boyfriends back and wrestled him to the floor he beat Bradley to death with his bare hands.

Gloria (baby girl) was so in tune to what Rashad was saying because she remembered when those two African brothers doped her mother up and beat and raped her so she knew exactly how Rashad felt because she killed the two brother's not with her bare hands but she empted her 9mm in both of them, before they could finish lunch baby girl decided to take Rashad's case and have a bond set for him to be released with a court date, baby girl told Rashad that her fee was going to be twenty five thousand to take his case and he need to give her ten thousand by the next day to even take him to the police station to turn him in.

Rashad told baby girl that he could pay her the whole amount because he didn't like not settling his debts he wrote her a check for twenty five thousand right then and handed to her, she liked his style because she always got paid in installments he was her first and she liked the fact that he was a business man, baby girl could see some of herself in Rashad she knew that he was a hard core killer but the only difference was he killed to protect his mother and she was a killer for hire.

Baby girl wrote all of his information down to run his name in her computer she called T.S.A.P. which she like to say To Serve And Protect her in her quest to find out information about her clients for her and her brother king, baby girl called that being equally yoked she felt that if she stayed on top of their clients information and their families whereabouts it was in their best interest, baby girl couldn't wait to get back to the office to fill Ava and Denise out on what their next case was going to be she knew by taking Rashad's case she was cutting it a little close.

Gloria (baby girl) found out that Brooklyn was a known drug
dealer and that he didn't have any children but he was known to be
a repeated offender, baby girl wanted to know more about Rashad
so she dug a little deeper because he peeked her interest, in her eye
sight this tall dark and handsome man had some hidden secrets that
she would soon find out that was very dark and dangerous, baby girl
was digging around in Rashad's world on her computer when she
ran across an article about this ten year old boy that set his house on
fire and his little sister was trapped and was burn alive in the fire,
the little girl was a pretty little girl with curly black her she was eight
years old and asleep when the house caught fire, the fire started in the
basement of the house because the ten year old boy was down in the
basement smoking dippers for those of you that don't know what that
it is it's marijuana rolled up and dipped in embalming fluid, a drug
that's used to embalm dead people another name for is called pcp.

This is a drug of confusion and it also has several different names
angel dust, crystal, hog, horse tranquilizer, and flakes, when baby girl
finished reading the articles that was written up about Rashad she
couldn't believe all the things that he had been in evolved in, so not
only did he kill his mother's boyfriend he had also killed his sister
and had served ten years for doing so, now what she was worried
about was while Rashad was smoking angel dust had he become
schizophrenic, she did some research on the drug to see what side
affects it had so she would know what to expect from Rashad.

Baby girl found out a few of the side effects that's associated with the
drug pcp, it distorts perceptions of sight and sound and produces
feelings of detachment from the environment and self, most first time

users experience a " bad trip" and stop, low dosage effects including shallow breathing, flushing and profuse sweating, baby girl was so terrified of what she was reading until she stopped reading and shut her computer down, she thought to herself that she might have done a lot of things in her life time but drugs was never a choice of hers.

Baby girl told her partners Ava and Denise what she had found out about their new client Rashad so it won't be any surprises, she just didn't want them to judge him in his wrong doings because they themselves wasn't as pure as the driven snow themselves, plus she did have a lustful eye for Mr. Rashad herself but she wasn't going to rush into anything she was going to play this one by ear, Baby girl arranged to turn Rashad into the authorities the next day to make sure he wouldn't give her any excuse's she let him spend the night with her, but to be on the safe side she kept her 9mm close to her head under her pillow with one hand on the trigger her model was it's best to be safe than sorry.

Baby girl got up the next morning to see if her guest was still sleeping but to her surprise Rashad a.k.a. Brooklyn had been up hours before her he had took a shower and was now in the kitchen cooking both of them breakfast, the only thing she could say to Brooklyn was a man after my own heart he smiled when he heard her say that because he didn't realize that she was standing in the kitchen door, Brooklyn turned around and asked her if she was ready to eat she asked him to give her twenty minutes and she would be right out, while baby girl was in the shower Brooklyn fantasized about how would it feel to make love to her in the shower under warm and soapy water cascading down both of their bodies, and then he thought it could wait because he would have her in due time.

Once breakfast was over baby girl got dressed and her and Brooklyn headed down to the police station when she entered the police station the officer at the desk looked at her with envy in his eye's because he knew that she represented her attorney status very well, she told the officer at the front desk that she was there to turn in her client Rashad Peoples for the murder of Floyd Scott, the officer was looking at her like she bumped her head or something because they didn't have any information containing to the murder she was talking about, so the office asked her to wait on the bench until he could find out some information containing to the murder she was talking about.

The officer returned back to the front desk with question after question he wanted to know when and where the murder was committed and was it committed in the Chicago area, baby girl was so infatuated with Rashad she had totally forgot to asked him where the murder was committed, when she realized that was a crucial question she turned around to ask Brooklyn where the murder was committed at? He told her the murder was committed in Chicago two years ago, once Rashad ran the scenario down to the officer at the front desk he started to think back about how brutal the murder was the man had been beat to a pulp, his family had to have a close casket funeral because the man face was broken in a thousand pieces it was like who ever beat him must of had a licenses for boxing.

When the officer looked over at Rashad he called upstairs and alerted the detectives that they had a two year old homicide client downstairs, when the two officers from upstairs came down they couldn't believe that Rashad hid out for two years he even escaped the most wanted poster they had on TV. bulletins all over the country looking for him, the two detectives was shocked because his mother had spent a year in jail because she didn't want to turn her son in for protecting her, they took Rashad in the interrogation room to question him about the murder when he told them the same story his mother told them they still couldn't believe that he beat Floyd Scott to death with his bare hands.

Rashad was arrested for the murder of Floyd Scott he just wished his mother was still alive to see that he finally did the right thing by turning himself in for murdering Floyd Scott, he knew in his heart that she would be happy for him that now he could stop running from the long arm of the law, because in reality he was only doing what any young man would of done protecting his mother from an abusive boyfriend, Rashad's mother Veronica died in prison after only serving a year when the day came for her to be released they went into her cell to find her hanging from the top bunk with a sheet tied around her neck with her head to the side with her eyes wide open.

Baby girl went home after they charged Rashad with the murder she came back the next morning to go in front of the judge to get a bail set for Rashad, the judge wasn't going to set a bond for Rashad because he felt that if he ran for two years he may just as well run again so his bond was denied, baby girl knew that because Rashad

had ran so long that the judge would deny him a bond but she also knew that she was going to do everything possible to help get out of this jam he was in because she still believed that they were from the same side of the tracks that's what made them equally yoked

---

chapter thirteen

The Return Of Conner Amy's Son

Amy had been on the run from angel for years she also had a child by angel's brother St. Louis, Amy was one of the girl's that angel found living on the streets when she arrived in Chicago to take over the family business with her two brothers David and Dante, Angel had two of the six apartment complexes to run her drug business's out of but she took her drug game up a step to black marketing babies from pregnant women with nowhere to go, angel didn't know at the time that Amy was pregnant by her man slash brother St. Louis until this day she still doesn't know that her brother has a son that will soon be introduced to the carter clan, Conner was graduating from school in two weeks he had been asking his mother about his father since he was six years old, Amy would always come up with a different lie every time Conner would ask his mom about his father and to Conner that was getting a little old, he wanted answers and if his mother wasn't willing to tell him the truth he was going to find out on his own.

Conner had been sneaking around in his mother dresser draws when he ran across his birth certificate saying who his father was and that he was born in Chicago so Conner said to himself that's a start, after Conner's graduation he was going to Chicago to fine his absentee father he wanted to get to know him and find out why he wasn't around to show him all the things he needed to become a man, it was three weeks later when Conner packed up and headed to Chicago he didn't tell his mother because he didn't want her to worry about him, but he did leave her a letter explaining that he wanted to spread his wings for a while and for her not to worry he will be staying in touch with her, Amy had a very bad feeling where her son went but she knew one day that he would go looking for his father and she wanted so desperately to keep him away from angel's conniving ass.

Conner had grew into a very respectable and intelligent man and he didn't know why his father wouldn't want him in his life, what Conner didn't know was he was about to open a door to a very nasty and corrupted world surrounding his mother and father lives, he was going to open a can of worms that was going to send his life spiraling out of control, Conner arrived in Chicago as plan he got a room at the holiday inn for a month he figure that would be enough time to find his father and any other information he needed, after he checked in to the hotel he caught the bus to down town Chicago to a restaurant to get him something to eat while he was sitting there minding his business in walk's Royal the naborihood bigmouth, which everybody calls snitching ass Royal her mouth is like an old ass refrigerator can't hold shit, when she seen this Carmel skin green eyed guy sitting alone at a table by himself she had to make her way over to the table to strike up a conversation, she said hi my name is Royal you must be new in town because I haven't seen you around here before, Conner looked at Royal like she had a problem because he didn't remember inviting her to his table and he thought that she was bold as hell for doing so, so Conner thought to himself he probable could use her to his advantage maybe she might be able to point him in the right direction.

91

Royal kept telling Conner that he favor someone she used to know but she couldn't place the face yet but she promised him that she swear they could be twins, Conner smiled because his brain didn't deceive him as far as Royal goes because she might be on to something and he wasn't about to let her out of his sight as of yet, Royal sat at the table running her mouth with Conner like she had diarrhea at the mouth he didn't mind because maybe she might spit out some information he needed to hear, she let Conner know who the man was that was running the drug empire and she also let him know about baby girl and her click, she told him if he ever was in trouble and wanted a kick ass attorney baby girl was the one, she went on to tell Conner that she would fight for justice for your ass if you got the right price.

Conner thought to himself that this girl don't know me from Adam and she talking to me like she been knowing me forever, she surly can talk, I know that if she talk that much she will tell on a nigga quick, because Conner only met her for twenty minutes and she singing like a canary, Conner had to slow Royal down a little bit because she was talking so fast he knew half the shit she was talking about she had to be lying.

When Conner heard her say the name St. Louis she struck a nerve he knew that's what they called his father that's the only name he heard his mother ever say, so Conner knew for sure he was going to keep close tabs on Royal because for now, at least he had a clue that she knew his father or she might know someone that did, Conner was desperate to find out about his father he also wanted to know why his mother had so many secrets about her life while living in Chicago, before Royal and Conner could finish their conversation king and his entourage of soldiers came walking in the door, Conner asked Royal who was king she said remember when I said it was a guy that ran the drug empire, well that's him right there you not going to ever catch him alone he always travel with an army of nigga's.

Conner told Royal he don't looked too much older than I do, she said remember the attorney I told you about she's his sister, Conner couldn't believe what he was hearing you telling me that king is a drug dealer and his sister is an attorney? Royal looked at Conner and said that's right she is, Conner said well they keeping shit pretty tight then aren't they, Royal said you better believe it, Royal started running off at the mouth again telling Conner that king ran six complex's and two other dope house's on the side, she said that nigga is nigga rich shit he makes enough money to burn.

Conner was sitting there thinking with his mine in overdrive he was thinking about joining kings crew not knowing that in order to get in kings crew you had to show loyalty by killing someone first, when Royal looked in Conner's direction he was deep in thought so she asked him was he ready to leave he asked her what she meant, she said I thought that maybe you wanted to spend some time with me he said baby I don't know you for real you might be trying to set me up or something, she said why would I do that I like you, why do you think I put you up on the game plan of who's who around here.

Conner like her style but he didn't trust anyone even though he was still a virgin he thought that it wouldn't be nothing wrong with Royal taking his virginity, so he invited Royal back to his hotel room before

93

they could make it in the room good Royal was coming out her clothes quicker than a hooker in whore house, Conner was excited because he only seen naked woman in magazines but to be up close and personal was something else for Conner his penis raised to the occasion immediately, he was more than ready he just didn't know what to do until Royal showed him what to do and he was more than ready to oblige her in her quest, Royal showed Conner shit that he had never seen in real life before she turned Conner young ass out she went from the doggie style position to sitting down in a chair in the toilet stool position Conner was smiling like a chipmunk eating a nut.

Once the love making session was over Royal and Conner laid in bed holding each other she started pillow talking to Conner telling him everything that was going on in the Chicago area, she even went back to telling him that St. Louis was the head nigga in charge before he got killed, when Conner heard the word killed he couldn't breathe his heart was pacing fast he wanted to kill whoever was responsible for the death of his father St. Louis, Royal knew what she said to Conner might have started him to breathing hard but she couldn't figure out why it affected him that way, so she couldn't help but ask him why was he so interested in St. Louis death, so Conner broke down and told Royal that he was his father.

Royal told Conner that she was sorry that he had to find out that his father was dead the way that he did and that she would do everything she could to help him find out who was responsible, the next day before Royal left Conner's room he asked her did she know anyone by the name of Amy Stonewell she said I don't think so but the name does sound familiar, I'll ask around in the hood to see what's up and I will let you know what I find out later on today is that cool" Conner said that was cool so she kissed him on the jaw and left, but before she could make it to the elevator she remembered she hadn't given Conner her cell number so she went back knocked on the door to give Conner her cell number.

Royal did go back in the hood to check out what Conner asked her to do and she did turn up with some good information, Royal found out that Conner's mother Amy was a runaway and a drug addict she stayed on the streets for a while until St. Louis got her off the streets, she stayed with him for a while until he kicked her out because she was stealing his product's but she didn't know she was pregnant by him until month's later even then she still didn't tell him she was carrying his child so St. Louis never knew about his son Conner, Royal also told Conner St. Louis had a daughter she remember the trial when angel was arrested for the Russian mafia murders St. Louis was always in the courtroom holding his baby girl, she told Conner if he wanted to find his sister that she would be more than happy to help him find her.

chapter fourteen

King Becoming A Dad

— •●• —

King and Aphrodite had been screwing each other like rabbits they stayed in the bed so much until Aphrodite hadn't notice that she was late for her visit for that time of the month until she tried on a pair of jeans she hadn't wore in a while, she tried to pull her jeans up over her legs when they stopped at her knees, she thought to herself I know I haven't gained any weight but my breast have gotten a little plump she told herself that she was going to stop at the drug store to pick up a pregnancy test on her way back from visiting her mother, once Aphrodite made it to her mother's house she knew right away that her daughter was pregnant, she told her daughter that she was beautiful and that she was glowing she looked at her mother wondering what in the world was she was talking about saying she was glowing, she asked her mother why did she say she was glowing? she said because my baby is having her own baby Aphrodite could have been knocked over with a feather because she really didn't think she was pregnant she just thought that by her and her man eating out so much might of picked up a little weight.

Her mother told her she was sure she was pregnant because she had two heartbeats in her neck to prove it, Aphrodite said mother please there you go when those old school saying's again she said if you think I'm lying to you let's go down to Walgreens to get a couple of those pregnancy test then, she agreed with her mother because she really wanted to find out for herself if she was carrying a child, Aphrodite and her mother picked up the pregnancy test and went back to her apartment and opened them up she told her daughter that she had to pee on the stick to get the results in about two minutes, Aphrodite did what her mother told her to do, while they were waiting she was thinking about what will king say about their new arrival, two minutes had passed and she was going back in the bathroom to get the pregnancy stick when she ran into her mother in the hallway, she said mom I'm too scared to find out what the results are will you please look at it for me and tell me what it say.

When Aphrodite's mother picked up the stick and it read positive she was smiling like she won a brand new car she was happy that she finally was going to be a grandmother, Aphrodite still wasn't sure she asked her mother was she sure she said of course I'm sure if you need more clarification let's go down to the free clinic, Aphrodite wanted to be one hundred percent sure before she confronted her man about their expected child, once her and her mother made it to the clinic she had two people ahead of her when they finally called her name she almost jumped out of her skin, her mother knew that she was nervous but she acted like she was afraid of something and she was going to find out what had her daughter so jumpy.

When the nurse ran Aphrodite's blood test and her urine test they both came back positive so Aphrodite was defiantly pregnant she was two months pregnant to be exact, she was happy that she was pregnant she just hoped that king felt the same way she did, she had just turned twenty five and king had just turned twenty, she had given herself a time limit of twenty five before she had a child now it was time to go face king with the good news, she was a little scared but it didn't matter to her how he excepted them having a child because she was going to have her baby anyway.

Aphrodite ate lunch with her mother before she returned back home when she returned home and walked in the front door she could hear king on the phone cursing somebody out about some money so she didn't know if it was a good time to tell him about the baby, so she decided against it for now but she knew she would have to tell him soon because she would be showing soon, when king realize that Aphrodite was home he shut his conversation off he didn't like bringing his madness around her because he knew she didn't like the life style he was living, when he looked at his woman and seen the worried look she had on her face he wanted to know what was up with her, so he asked her was she alright? she said yes I'm fine but we need to talk king said alright but can we talk tonight because I have some business I need to handle right now, she said fine and he went out the door leaving Aphrodite at home with food for thought why did I let him leave without tell him about our baby.

King knew it was some heavy shit on Aphrodite's mine he could tell but he didn't time right then nor did he have time to listen to what she had to say right then, but he did make a mental note to finish what he was doing and get back home to hear what his girl was trying to tell him, when king made it to king towers and chewed out his soldier for throwing his product away because the police rolled up on him, he made sure to let him know that this week's pay will be deducted out of his pocket for being so stupid in carrying that shit on him, king finished blowing off steam in an hour he told his right hand man Dallas that he wanted to go back to his crib to talk with his girl, once he made it to his crib he found Aphrodite sitting in the kitchen crying with a big bowel of chocolate chip ice-cream he ran straight to her because something really bad had to be wrong for his girl to be sitting there crying.

King grabbed Aphrodite around the waist and pulled her up from the chair he wrapped his arms around her pulling her into his chest he wanted to know why was she so upset, she told king every time I want to have a talk with you, you don't have time this is serious king and I think we need to talk about this, he told her alright baby my time is all yours let's talk ok I'm sorry if I made you cry I didn't do it intentionally, when Aphrodite looked up at king he felt that he really did something to hurt her and he wanted to know what he had done so bad to make her cry, she couldn't wait to spit it out she said you might need to sit down he stopped looked at her and said why you going to leave me or something? She said no I'm not but I am adding on an addition to our family, king was dumbfounded to what she had just said he said excuse me, she said king we are having a baby before she could say anything else king picked her straight up in the air he was screaming we going to have a Shorty she said yes baby we are.

King was so happy about the baby that he was telling anyone that would listen he forgot to tell one person and that was his sister baby girl, so he thought that him and his girl should tell her together so he called her and invited her over for dinner he also told her to bring her son smoke with her, baby girl was like it's something going on with my brother because he never asked me to bring my son with me, when she hung up with king she called her house to make sure her son was there so she could swing by and pick him up but as usually he didn't answer, when she went home after work to change into some more comfortable clothes she heard moaning coming from her basement smoke was down there cracking some girls back, she went down the stairs with a broom she told the girl to get dressed and get the hell out her house and don't come back, she looked at her son she and as far as you go get your black ass upstairs to your room and don't come out I'll talk to you when I get back smoke I can't believe you had the damn nerve to disrespect my house like that.

Baby girl was so pissed with smoke she couldn't hardly talk when she made it to kings condo when she knocked on his door and he opened it he could tell she had been crying, he hugged his sister he had to asked what was wrong when she told him she busted smoke screwing in her basement he just smile he said relax sis he's at that age were he's exploring things, she said exploring my ass I'm too young to be a grandmother and he's not going to keep disrespecting me in my damn house either you need to talk to him before I beat his ass king, king promised his sister that he will have a sit down with smoke tomorrow and to stop worrying he will take care of it, she said I'll let you take care of it but trust and believe that, that boy is on his last leg with me, when Aphrodite came in the living room to tell them that dinner was ready baby girl notice the glow on her face she said oh shit y'all having a baby, I'm going to be an aunt Aphrodite said you are going to be an aunt baby girl said I wish mommy was here she would be so proud of you, so that you know I'm going to give the biggest baby shower you ever seen I'm going to put it in the news paper as well my niece or nephew is going to have everything money can buy.

When baby girl was through bragging on her brothers baby she started thinking about how disrespectful her son had became he acted like he hated her and she was going to get to the bottom of smoke's behavior toward her, king had smoke best interest at heart but he wasn't going to stand by and let him disrespect his sister by no means, so he decided to go over to baby girls house as promise to talk with his nephew he wanted him to get his shit together before he had to stick his foot up his ass about his sister, when smoke opened the door and seen king he knew it wasn't just a social visit he knew his mother went and told that nigga what went down with him getting busted in her basement.

Smoke was mad that king call his self coming over to his crib checking him about something his mother said, he let his uncle get what he had on his chest off but deep down inside smoke didn't give a damn about what king was saying, because as far as he was concern baby girl and king was out for themselves he never came into their equation until he was doing something wrong, king decided that it was time to take his nephew under his wing that way he could keep a close eye on him and try to keep him out of trouble, smoke wanted to be just like his uncle and he knew that if he spent a lot of time with him one day he could be sitting on king's throne.

------•------

chapter fifteen

Darcey And Olympia

———————•◉•———————

Olympia was feeling a little bit under the weather she was still missing that void that fueled her life she still wasn't able to give her husband that one thing he wanted most in his life a child, but she did have her sister that kept her on her toes for the most part, Olympia and her husband still wanted Darcy to carry their child as they agreed upon and she was more than happy to do it, they had been to so many fertility clinics trying to make sure that Darcy got pregnant but for some reason they eggs would die and that made Olympia want to give up, the day that she told her husband that they were fighting a losing battle, right when she broke down crying the phone started ringing it was Dr. Benito asking them if they could come to his office and to bring Darcy with them, when they arrived at the doctor's office he was sitting behind his desk reading their file he said I need you guy's to have a seat because I have some great news to tell you about your last visit here, Olympia was sitting there with her eyes bucked because she just knew it was going to be bad news even after the doctor said it was good news, the doctor said I'm glad to tell you the last in fertility test we did came out positive you my dear Darcy is carrying a healthy set of twins, before he could congratulate the couple and Darcy all he could hear was cries of happiness the room was filled with nothing but happiness.

Olympia was so over whelmed with joy until she thank her sister
over and over for what she was doing for her and her husband, Darcy
had made her sister the happiest woman in the world she wasn't just
carrying one baby for her she was carrying two, Olympia was going
to spoil her sister to death she was also going to be with her at every
doctor's appointment, the trio was so excited when they left the
doctor's office until they couldn't think straight all they could think
about was shopping for the twins, when they went to the mall to
the baby store they seen a double stroller that they just had to buy,
Douglas looked at Darcy because he was so proud of her for helping
them out by carrying their child he could also see that she was tired
so they left the mall and headed back to their house so she could get
some much needed rest, when they made it home Darcy went straight
to bed she sleep thru the night like an infant.

The next morning she was still asleep when she was woke up by her
sister a breakfast fit for a queen, her sister had already started to give
Darcy the royal treatment, they had another doctor's appointment
in two weeks to make sure everything was going smoothly with the
twins so until then Olympia was at home pampering her sister to the
fullest, she was putting pillow's under her swollen feet and prompting
them up and the whole nine yards.

Douglass on the other hand was spoiling her to but he wasn't treating
her like she was handicap like her sister was doing, he knew Darcy
knew how to take care of herself he just had to make sure that his
wife knew that as well, one night they all were asleep when Olympia
started screaming in her sleep she had a dream that the babies was
drowning in their placenta bag she kept saying get my babies their

drowning somebody help me please, Douglas jumped up and started shaking Olympia to weak her up when Darcy came in the room she heard her sister screaming from her bedroom she thought that she was having a bad dream about angel, Douglas and Darcy assured her that the babies was fine and that was only a bad dream she was a having.

The days was passing by like minutes and the weeks was passing like hours before they knew it was time to go see Dr. Benito, when the trio arrived at his office he was ready to give Darcy her first ultrasound she was greased up and ready to get pictures of the babies, when Dr. Benito turn on the machine and put the ultrasound to work they could see the twins holding on to each other when he started rubbing around Darcy stomach they started to move where he could see to determine what the sex of the twins were, when he told the trio that they were having a boy and a girl they jumped for joy because it didn't matter what they were as long as they were healthy.

The babies were to be born in seven months and Olympia couldn't wait to for their arrival she was so excited until she couldn't stop talking about dressing up the nursery, she was thinking about colors and baby equipment to dress the nursery with she was even going to call in a decorator to design the nursery, Douglass was happy to but he didn't want his wife with her hopes up to high before Darcy got into her second trimester of pregnancy, Darcy and Olympia was sitting around talking one night when the conversation about paying angel a visit once the twins was born, because they didn't want angel to ever come after the twins if she was to get wind that Olympia had children, they thought back to the killing they done to the Sanchez brother's and how baby girl was heartless like her mother, and yes they help set the stage but to burn them alive was all baby girl's doing, Olympia said in order for us to kill angel we have to go after baby girl, Ava and Denise you know they tied at the hip with angel and her daughter so we have to come up with the perfect plan to kill of all of them.

While they were in the bedroom talking Douglas had come home and was standing outside the bedroom door listening to what they were saying about angel and baby girl, then out of know where Darcy said she's going to pay for beating you like she did and burning my face and hair off my head, Douglas was frozen stiff he couldn't believe that any one human had a conscious that was that brutal to do what she did to Darcy and Olympia, and to think she was a female at that, Douglas wanted to make sure his wife stayed as far away from angel as possible, because if angel could do the damage she did to them the first time only god knows what she will do next time if they crossed paths with her again.

Douglas wasn't going to let the sister go after angel because what he seen them go through was horrible something he wasn't going to bring them back from if they went up against her again, to him angel should be hogged tied and gutted because she didn't have a heart or a soul, that was just the way Douglas was thinking because he didn't have a bad bone in his body, just hearing how angel toured Darcy and Olympia made Douglas sick to his stomach, he dropped his medical bag by the door and ran to the bathroom it was beyond him how a female could be so cold and dangerous.

He got himself together and went into their bathroom to take a shower once in the shower Douglas was standing under the hot water letting it cascade down his head and shoulders when he felt someone's hand sliding down his back it was Olympia she had joined him in the shower without Douglas knowing she had entered the shower, he was so deep in thought about the tragedy that Darcy and Olympia had been through until he hadn't process the shower door sliding open.

He turned around and seen his wife standing there naked and the water hitting up against her skin and all he could think about was running his tongue over her now erect breast, they were about to have sex in the shower sex in the water is going to be very exciting and intense Douglass introduce Olympia to a bubbly back float, Douglas knew this position well he gives pelvic flexibility you can experiment with, with both of their pelvis rubbing together, he started soaping her up and just slide his hands up and down and around until he reaches her clitoris adding extra sensation, he started kissing down her next he pulled her legs apart put one on his shoulder to get a good angel of penetration he was creating an alternating sensation for her, he was rocking with an intensifying affect that was sending Olympia to an orgasm she would never forget, Olympia was screaming so loud in the shower she woke Darcy up and the only thing Darcy could do was smile wishing she could do the same thing.

---

chapter sixteen

Gloria (Baby Girl 'S) New Man Rashad A.K.A. Brooklyn

———•———

Gloria (baby girl) was thinking about Brooklyn like crazy she had even started having sexual dreams about him and he haven't even be released from jail yet, she was so into this man that she hardly knew but she did know one thing he was heavy on her mine and in her dreams she wanted him, he was her type of guy with a hard and rugged edge, she was going to pay Brooklyn a visit today in jail she didn't have to talk to him about his case because she knew what was going on with his case frontwards and backwards, she just wanted to go and see her secret lover up close and personal, making visit that she loved drooling while she watched him.

When baby girl made it to the jail she was dressed to kill she had on this dress made of sheer that was see thru she knew she wasn't supposed to be dressed that way but she was trying to make a statement to Brooklyn that she wanted him to have her in the most satisfying way, when Brooklyn walked in the waiting room looking like he had been pumping iron out on the yard, he had picked up a few pounds and it was most definitely showing thru his shirt he was getting ripped and baby girl was getting hot and bothered just looking at him, the guards at the jail had never seen an attorney come and visit their client everyday like baby girl did they started standing around whispering because they thought that it was odd that she seen Brooklyn everyday it through up all kinds of red flags in their book.

Baby girl watched the guards go on the defense but she didn't give a damn she was there for Brooklyn not them so if they had beef with her they needed to address her with whatever they were saying until then they could kiss where the sun didn't shine, her and Brooklyn was sitting at one of the tables when he asked baby girl was there anything she needed to tell him? She said no I just came to see if you were doing alright he looked at her and smiled, he said you know I see you every day and you going to sit here and tell me it's about my well being, she said that's it I'm on top of seeing to it that you are doing fine up in this terrible place, Brooklyn told her that you not fooling me because I know the real reason why you are here every day, you stuck on a nigga but if you want to keep lying to yourself so be it, but believe me you and I are emotionally attached to each other so you need to stop playing girl, she looked at Brooklyn smiling because he had just put the nail in the coffin.

When she finally left the jail they had established what they were going to do as for as their relationship status, she went there for him to bring out what she couldn't the way she really felt about him, now that she's going to be Brooklyn's woman slash attorney they were going to love being bed buddies, she was giddy all the way home knowing that once Brooklyn makes it home she was going to put it on him because thinking about how they were going to do it wasn't enough she wanted to be penetrated, she went to bed that night once again with Brooklyn on the brain she was dreaming about a karma sutra position she had in mind that she wanted to try with Brooklyn, she was just hoping that she wasn't looked at as being freaky but then again she said the hell with it I wouldn't care what he thought as Horney as I am.

Baby girl woke up out her sleep because she heard a loud crash outside her window when she jumped up to go to the window it was her neighbor next door, he was drunk and he had knock the trash can up on her curve she was pissed because he had fucked up a good dream she was just about to get mounted by Brooklyn, it took baby girl a while to go back to sleep so she went into the kitchen to get her a glass of wine so she could wind down some, but what she didn't know was she wasn't going to wind down she was going to wind up because Brooklyn was deeper in her thoughts than she thought, Brooklyn was branded in her brain like a tattoo he was creeping through her mind like crazy, it was like they both had extra sensory perception because why she was thinking of having sex with Brooklyn he was laying in his bunk thinking the same thing, so the feeling's were mutual Brooklyn had baby girl in his mind buck naked scrolled a crossed the kitchen table getting ready to be served up like a Christmas turkey she would have been his Christmas dinner and desert all in one meal.

Baby girl finally made it back to bed as soon as she closed her eyes she went back into her loved fest dream of Brooklyn, she had her friend in her dresser draw right next to the bed she knew he could do the job because she bought him extra large, she also had a name picked out for it she called him big horse, baby girl was working horse all the while she was thinking about Brooklyn she was getting wet ejaculating like a women going to death row she was getting off so good she said to herself that she could be a porno queen, mean while why she was working horse Brooklyn was working snake that's what he called his penis because he had the length but he was a little short on the width.

Baby girl was on her way to work the next morning when she received a phone call on her cell saying that she had to get to the prison quick she made a u-turn and headed to the prison, it took her twenty minutes to get there once she got checked in she asked the guard behind the desk what was going on he told her to wait and talk to the warden, all she could think about was something had happen to Brooklyn and if it did heads was going to roll, once the warden came out to escort baby girl to his office in the back he explained to her that Brooklyn had gotten into a fight with another inmate in the yard and that he had gotten stabbed and was on his way to the hospital, she told the warden why the hell did you call me all the way out here if he was on his way to the hospital that was really stupid don't you think, the warden looked at her like he wanted to slap the shit out of her but he knew if he did he would have a law suit on his hands, baby girl didn't have nothing else to say so she turned around and left going over to the hospital to see how bad of shape Brooklyn was in, when she made it there they had to guards posted up outside Brooklyn's hospital door.

When she showed the guards her identification they let her into the room when she looked at Brooklyn laying in the bed asleep she wanted to cry because he looked so helpless with his stomach all bandaged up, she just grabbed his hand and said a prayer right when she finished praying Brooklyn opened his eye's he asked her why was she there and who told her that he was in the hospital? She told him she had gotten a call from the warden and he called her because she was down on his emergency list as his next of kin, he said that's right I did put you down for my emergency call if anything was to happen to me she said alright mister funny man what happen to you? He told baby girl he was in the yard playing basketball when this want to be drug dealer came up to him in the yard and said he heard from another inmate that he was talking shit about his product.

Baby girl told Brooklyn don't you think that was some petty shit, now you laying up in the hospital on some he said shit, that's not cool at all Brooklyn he said I know but that nigga is going to pay for stabbing me so the warden better make sure he separate us once I get back there, baby girl said you will be separated because you are being transferred Brooklyn because I'm not going to lose you over no bull-shit alright, Brooklyn told her if you get me transferred that's going to make me look like I'm scared and that's not my style girl, she said don't get it twisted I know you not scared but I don't want you caught up in another murder before I can get this one cleared up you feel me, Brooklyn knew what she was saying but he also knew he never back down from a fight he didn't give a damn who the person was.

He agreed to be transferred because of baby girl so she could rest peacefully at night knowing that she would be okay made his transfer more easy, baby girl though that Brooklyn was all hers she didn't know that he had a crazy ass ex he left behind in new York while he was hiding out from the police, this girl was a crazy ass psychotic fool for real she would stalk Brooklyn for day in and day out, that girl

111

even killed a squirrel and nailed it to his front door of his apartment, she told him nigga I'm in love with you and you just want to up and leave me, I don't think so because if you think that you are going to come into my life make me fall in love with you and you just going to throw me to the curve like a old ass news paper darling you sadly mistaking, let's just keep it real I have stayed in a mental institution for two years they classified me as mentally crazy so if I killed your black ass right now there wouldn't be a damn thing they could do to me but put my crazy ass back in the hospital where I should have stayed, now it's up to you what's it's going to be?

Brooklyn at the time didn't know when he met Skye she had just been released from a mental institution, he was trying to break up with Skye Henderson he didn't know she was crazy he had no idea she had been institutionalized until that day he was trying to let her down easy, while baby girl was in the hospital visiting Brooklyn Skye had been sitting in the hospital waiting area when baby girl walked in she said to herself I know this ass—hole didn't stop seeing me to see the next bitch, so she waited on baby girl to come out of Brooklyn's room to leave, she followed baby girl home from the hospital that night she did the unthinkable she waited to baby girl got out of her car and went into her house she slid under her car and cut her break-line to her brand new Mercedes.

The next day baby girl didn't feel right it was like she knew something was wrong so she didn't drive her Mercedes to work the next morning she drove her BMW instead, Skye stayed outside baby girl's house all night she wanted to know who the hell this female is hanging around her man, when Skye seen baby girl come out and get into a different car she was pissed because she wanted to kill her quick she didn't want to wait she was in the way of her winning back her man, when baby girl got to work she told Ava and Denise that she felt weird like someone was tailing her but she didn't recognize the car, but it was someone definitely following her because that same car was sitting outside her house when she came out this morning and now it was sitting across the street from her office, she said whoever this person is their crazy to follow me from my house and now their sitting across the street from my job I think I'm going over to their car, Ava you and Denise gear up because I'm going to teach this fool a lesson they're not going to forget any time soon.

When baby girl and her crew came out of her office and headed across the street Skye pulled off she was going so fast until she ran the red light right in front of the police they pulled her over three blocks away, she had to think of a good explanation because she was caught dead to right with running that red light, Skye told the police that she had a real bad tooth ache and she had just took her medicine and she was trying to get back to her hotel room before the medicine kicked in, she was smart because she had even put a ball of tissue in her jaw to make it look swollen so she could get the officers sympathy, the officer asked Skye was she visiting the Chicago area because the car she was driving had New York plates she said no I stay here in Chicago this is my cousin's car and she made up a name but she gave him baby girl's address, the officer did feel sorry for Skye and let her off with a warning he told her to go home and not to run any more red light's she told the officer she was going straight home and go to bed, the officer was so messed up by looking at Skye's right jaw being swollen until he didn't ask her for her driver's licenses or insurance card, Skye was lucky that night because she would have spent a night in jail because she had New York credentials, when the officer pulled off behind Skye she went right back to baby girl's house because the officer followed her back there to make sure she made it home safely, Skye got out the car like she was really going into the house so the officer pulled off and waved his hand to let her know that he was gone.

Skye said these some stupid ass police here in Chicago I think I'm going to stay around a while to check things out and make sure my man is not forgetting what I said before he left town, Skye also thought about getting to know baby girl on a personal level that way she would know how to handle her ass to.

The next day Skye decided to go rent her a car that way she can walk right up in baby girl's office for some legal advice and meet her nemesis in person, she wanted to know what this bitch had that she didn't that Brooklyn had to bring his ass all the way to Chicago with this bitch, what Skye had to do next was look the part of a female that was married to a high profile rich man that was abusive to her.

Skye went to the mall and purchased her three suit's that was at least fifteen hundred dollars apiece she then went to buy shoes and accessories that went with her wardrobe, after shopping at the mall for two hours she went to the beauty salon and had her hair dyed and straighten out into a long wrap she was flawless when she came out of the salon, she stopped by the nail salon and had her nails done also Skye knew she looked like a million bucks when she left up out of the hair salon.

Skye was coming out of the nail salon when a guy passing by said damn baby where your man at he must be crazy letting an angel like you go out by herself, she looked at the man like he was crazy and kept stepping he said oh you one of those stuck up bitches she told him to go fuck his self and she kept it moving, in Sykes mind she didn't have time for him she was on a mission and he wasn't in her plans.

chapter seventeen

King's Soldiers

———————•••———————

King wanted to have a little R and R with his soldiers lately things had been feeling a little out of whack so he wanted to take them out of their environment for a little fun, king knew how it was to be in business mode all the time so he thought it was time for a little adjustment because his soldiers were always on high alert, club sexy was jumping when they arrived at the club so even thou they were there to loosen up and have fun they still watched each other's backs, king was still feeling some kind of way about bow legs he would always come up missing in action when it was time for meetings and other things like them going to the club to unwind, king told Dallas that it's some shady shit going on with that nigga bow legs man he's been acting out of character every since you and your brothers came on the set.

Dallas told king well you know what maybe we should check out what's really going on I thinks it's better to know than to just sit back and have assumptions about what he's doing, to be honest he has been giving us shade since we got here so just maybe he has a wild hair up his ass that needs to be snatched out, king sole heartily agreed with what Dallas was saying because it did look like bow legs was definitely falling back from king and his soldiers.

That night when the action at the club came into full swing Bow legs came walking in the door it took everything in king's power not to snatch a knot in bow legs ass, he just thought to himself that he would wait until the club closed but he was definitely going to check his ass after they got back to kings towers, bow legs seen the way king was watching him he knew his ass was going to be in a sling as soon as they made it back to kings towers. bow legs couldn't enjoy his self because he knew he was up to know good he was playing with fire and he was the one that was going to get burned, an hour before the club closed king went over to bow legs to ask him why was he always missing in action so much king couldn't wait to ask him why, He had gotten drunk and his mind was on overload he was tired of bow legs making him look like a chump in front of his soldiers.

Bow legs knew he had to come up with something that made king believe him or else so he came up with a good lie about this honey he met that got pregnant by him that's been keeping him tied up, king knew bow legs was lying because why now this honey just now showing up something wasn't right with that picture so he decided to put a couple of his soldiers on watch duty, he wanted bow legs ass watched for now on because he knew when he smelt a rat and bow legs proved to be a stinking ass rat no doubt, king told Dallas that there comes a time when you have to say when enough is enough, but only you will know when that is and it's time you" feel me" Dallas told king yeah I feel you, the problem is with some people is that we are mistaken for bikes and are used for kickstands but that fool will soon find out that kickstands even get kicked out from underneath your ass too.

Bow legs couldn't shake the feeling that king and Dallas was sitting there looking and talking about him he knew that they were deep in thought because their body language that they were sending off was powerful toward him, king was throwing all kinds of shade toward bow legs he was going to find out what was behind that mask he was wearing, king didn't like the way he was feeling because he had too much at stake to have a snake in his camp and it wasn't going to be long before he discovered who the snake was and chop his head off, bow legs really did have a honey that he was seeing name Kay he was seeing but she wasn't the one taking his time he was sneaking around being a informant for the feds quiet as kept, king had two of his soldiers Juice and Bryce to eye their eyes on bow legs he want to know when bow legs took a shit in the mornings so they had to be on a twenty four hour detail in watching bow legs every move.

King was telling the brothers Dallas, Diego and Detroit that if that nigga bow legs is foul we going to teach his ass a lesson that he himself haven't even heard of for "sho" and that's real talk you "feel me" there's nothing worse than a crab ass snitching ass nigga, the brothers agreed because they knew from experience when it's a rat in your camp and he smiling in your face like he's clean as cotton knowing all the time he's info trading your secrets back to the law, bow legs didn't know what to do because he was caught in a trap for the feds plus he owed them cats in Michigan big money either way his life was coming to a serious end fast.

While bow legs was trying to figure out a way to get out of this mess he had put himself in he was smoking crack cocaine like it was going out of business, he started having a hallucinations thinking about

how he could kill that nigga king and take over his empire, he started
to get angry because king was a young nigga you could still smell
formula on his breath and he come to town and just took the fuck
over that shit didn't sit well with bow legs at all he was pissed off at
the fact that king ran shit, bow legs was so high that he didn't even
notice he that he had a tail on him for three days, Juice and Bryce
watched bow legs rent a hotel room to get high in he might have had
a girlfriend but he had a better girlfriend that was keeping him high
that he loved the most and she was called cocaine.

Bow legs was so busy getting high until he had missed the time to go
holler at king, king had called him twice to come by so they could
talk but bow legs didn't answer his cell, when he was getting high he
didn't give a damn about anybody the only thing that matter to him
was sucking on that glass pipe, which one would call a glass dick, king
put in a call to Bryce and Juice to find out if they were still on Bow
legs trail? They told king yes they were and he was stashed up inside
the Days inn hotel sucking on that glass dick king said you mean to
tell me that nigga in there smoking up my shit, Bryce told king I'm
tell you again I had been telling you that Bow legs is an undercover
smoker for a while look at his skin he appearance has changed
drastically, he don't even dress like he use to that nigga walking
around here like the walking dead.

King got directions to the hotel where Bow legs was stashed up in
and headed to the hotel he was more than pissed when he made it
to the hotel, he met Bryce and Juice on the parking lot when he said
what room is he in they told him he was on the fourth floor in room
410, when king started to go to the room he had a premonition he

knew if Bow legs seen him at the door he wasn't going to answer it, so he asked the maid at the hotel if she wanted to make two hundred dollars by doing him a favor, by knocking on the door for a room service visit, she knew he had a do not disturb on the door so she would be taking a chance by knocking on the door, she took the two hundred dollars from king and knocked on the door anyway. when Bow legs peeped out the peep hole he seen a vision of an angel in his high induced mine and opened the door, what he saw next took him by surprise it was the devil in kings image his eye's got as big as bow dollars he was scared shitless, because he knew if king ever found out he was smoking up his product that the after math behind it was going to be dangerous, king told the maid she could leave and went in the room and closed the door behind him, the maid was scared for the guy in the room because if something happened to him she would be responsible for going to his room and knocking on the door getting him to open it knowing he had a do not disturb notice on his door, that would be means of a automatic termination of her job plus questioning by the police of why she let a killer in the room in the first place.

King looked at Bow legs with discussed in his eyes he didn't want to believe that his first lieutenant was a dope head, he told Bow legs I'm glad I didn't put my faith in your sorry ass and to think that you was going to pull the wool over my eyes was a big mistake partner, now let me ask you a question before I put a bullet in your ass what made you think that I wasn't going to find out about your drug problem? Bow legs told king I didn't, no one knew I was stressed out and the only thing that could make me stay on top of things was staying high, I didn't think that you would ever find out for real now that you know what's up, I didn't want you to find out this way I was going to tell you once I got my nerves up to tell you, I didn't want to be kicked off the crew for being high all the time, king told Bow legs he knew about his disposition with the nigga's in Michigan he also told him he knew he owed them money and how much he owed them, Bow legs wasn't surprised by kings finding because he knew that king checked your ass out like the federal bureau of investigations, king looked at Bow legs one more time before he said you know what time it is don't you? It's time for me to cancel your contract Bow legs said king I'm so sorry young blood I won't do it again, king told him I know you won't because today will be your last time bending me over fucking me without any grease player and that's real talk.

King told Bow legs go on and get your last high because you will be going to hell fucked up so when you see my nigga satin tell him I'm catch up with him later, Bow legs took that glass dick put it in his mouth and fired it up in his mind he said he might as well go out in a blaze of glory, king sat there until Bow legs smoked up all the product he had on him, while Bow legs was sitting there smoking king texted messaged the twins Kaylen and Keith he told them where to meet him and what room he was in he wanted them once again to prove their loyalty to him by killing Bow legs.

When the twins arrived at the hotel they spotted Bryce and Juice sitting on the parking lot that sent up their antennas but it didn't even faze them because they were ready for whatever was about to go down, they headed over to the car to speak to the their crew members when they received another text asking them where were they, they left the guys in the parking lot and went up to room 410 when king opened the door they seen Bow legs stretched out on the sofa with his head tilted to the side he looked like he was cracked the hell out, king gave orders for them to wake him up he wanted Bow legs looking at him when he gave the order for his demise.

Keith sat Bow legs up on the sofa he smacked the shit out of him to get him to open his eyes but in reality Bow legs was so far gone off that crack cocaine he wouldn't of notice if the hotel blew the hell up, he was already dead and they didn't know it because he had smoke enough cocaine to kill at least three other people, king told them to check his damn vitals when they did Bow legs was already gone to meet his maker in hell he took his last breath while king was texting the twins, king was disappointed because he didn't get a chance to send a message about fucking with his product.

---

chapter eighteen

Kings Sidekick Skye

———————•·•———————

King was having a good day so he decided to treat his self to a long over do shopping spree so he went into the mall ready to spend some money when this fine ass female caught his eye, king said to himself damn she almost as fine as my gal, she has way more ass than my girl she's much older than my girl too I'm go holla" at her just to see what's up with "ma", king went up to the jewelry counter where Skye was standing pretending like she wanted to purchase a watch when she looked over at him she said damn young blood is fine damn, king noticed her watching him so he said what's up ma", Skye said sweetie I'm not down with that Ebonics okay you come at me correct or don't come at all alright, and let's get something straight I'm not your mother.

King said damn you go straight for the throat don't you she said I'm not for playing games sweetie the last gentleman I dated wind out in the cemetery for playing with my feelings, he said alright I can dig where you coming from, so first let me introduce myself to you my name is Ramon but everyone calls me king, Skye said my name is Skye but I still don't get why people call you king I don't see any crown on your head, king started laughing because he thought that she was so cute with her trying to play hard to get game so he played along just for fun.

King invited Skye out for lunch at one of the food courts he thought that would be a good time to find out a little something about Ms. Skye, Skye told king he had a beautiful smile and she asked him why was he at the mall? And was he there just looking for a hook up with some potential females? King said it's not even like that "ma", you telling me that a brother can't come to the mall just to shop, Skye told king of course men shop but men are hunters they also hunt for female's also.

King looked at Skye and said I don't run around town to different mall's looking for female's because look at me I'm a brother that has what it takes to pull any female I desire, Skye liked King's style because he was more than sure of himself he was cocky and she ate that shit up because she seen some of Brooklyn in King, Skye was staring at King so hard until he asked her was something wrong? she said no there isn't I just admire your since of style I'm just trying to picture you in my bed, King smiled at Skye and said well you don't have to waste your time with pictures "ma" I'm right here in the flesh so what's up? King didn't know that Skye was using him as bait to get close to his sister she knew when King entered the mall that he was baby girl's brother because she had been following baby girl around for day's, she knew King was a heavy hitter she also knew his young ass was the man when it came to the drug game.

Skye thought to herself this young nigga has some clot around town he also has at least two or three soldiers with him at all times so now I know what time it is with him, so Skye thought it was time to put her plan in motion since King sister took her man she thought that she could hook King up in her trap of seduction, that way she could get close to baby girl and trap her and show her how it feels to take something that doesn't belong to you, in reality Skye had really lost her damn mine because Brooklyn didn't belong to her, Skye was determined to win Brooklyn back at all cost she even was willing to kill baby girl to win back the love of her life.

What Skye failed to realize was King wasn't her problem nor was baby girl Brooklyn was the one that lead her to believe that he was going to leave his wife and marry her, and she wasn't going to get what she was looking for as far as hurting baby girl trying seduce King because King had plans on just having sex with her and moving on his main concern was Aphrodite, Don't get it twisted he did like Skye but his heart was with the one he first laid eyes on the one who struck fire in his heart which was Aphrodite she had a twist in that ass that sent King ass on a level that he couldn't reach plus he was still a virgin because that little sex caper he had with precious wasn't shit compared to what he experience with Aphrodite.

Skye and King little lunch date they had at the food court at the mall was coming to an end when king received a phone call from one of his soldiers saying that one of his drug house's had been robbed, King told Skye he had some business to take care of and he had to bounce, but he did ask her for her seven digits so he could contact her later on that day.

Skye was more than happy to give King her number because she knew she was going to invite him over to her house that night to see if King really was the man in the sheets, she knew from the streets he was the man but time will tell if he could hold his own in her bed.

King was riding with his crew on the way back to his drug house when the subject came up about Skye Dallas told King she was fine but it was something about her that gave him the creeps, King told Dallas don't even trip because he planned on just doing a hit and miss with Skye that's all he wasn't trying to wife her he just wanted to see what it was like to go to bed with a cougar, they all started laughing because they knew King was going to have one hell of experience with Miss Skye.

King and his soldiers made it to his crack house in record time he wasn't surprise of the break in because he knew it was a inside job, so he called a meeting right then and there because somebody was going to tell him who took his shit, one of his soldiers that ran the house name Bingo wasn't anywhere to be found so King turned on his transmitter that he had the soldiers to wear when they wasn't where they suppose to be he would hit that transmitter and shock the shit out of them, when the meeting begin and everyone was accounted for but Bingo king knew then that Bingo ass was up to some shady shit, plus by king hitting that transmitter and he still hadn't shown up that meant to king that he found someone to disconnect the bracelet from his arm, because the way king had those bracelets hooked up it consist of two keys and didn't anyone have a key but him and his sister baby girl, any other way would take their wrist and hand clean off because it would blow up with the small amount of C4 he had added to the bracelets.

Trust and loyalty was something king was adamant about with his soldiers from the beginning if they couldn't go by his rules then they knew to keep it moving because he didn't have time for mistakes in the business he was in, when the meeting was over and King discovered that he lost a million dollars he went ballistic someone was going to pay for his drugs and money coming up missing and the way things look it was all blamed on Bingo, king put word out that if any one of his soldiers see Bingo he wanted them to call him a.s.a.p. he didn't even want Bingo to think that he was even looking for him he wanted to surprise Bingo.

Mean while Bingo was on the other side of town getting ready to have his bracelet removed from his wrist not knowing that it had C4 in it he felt the shock when King hit the transmitter, but he wasn't about to go back to the drug house knowing that his life was now in danger from robbing King of his product and money, Bingo told his cousin Logan that he was tired of making King nigger rich while they sit back and collect crumbs, Bingo said I'm tired of being that little nigga puppet on a string he pulling the damn string and we bouncing to his damn music today I decided it was time I made a few changes.

Bing and his cousin Logan couldn't cut the bracelet off so Logan went in the garage to retrieve a blow torch to burn the bracelet off, when Logan came back in the house with the blow torch Bingo asked him what the hell he thought he was going to do with the blow torch? Logan said Bingo we tried almost everything but this I don't think we have a choice, Bingo said you know I don't think we have a choice either but I don't trust that young nigga, isn't no telling what that fool have in these bracelets man for real, alright Logan man if we are going to burn this shit off I'm going to need a stiff drink so go in the kitchen and get that Hennessey, when Logan returned with the Hennessey Bingo took a big swallow and told Logan to fire up the blow torch, when the blow torch came to life Bingo started drinking more Hennessey when the blow torch hit Bingo's wrist the bracelet blew up Bingo and his cousin died on impact the blow torch was still burning and the whole house caught on fire, the boom was so loud that the neighbors call the fire department when they arrived to put the fire out it was two unedifying bodies in the house burned to a crisp.

When Logan's girlfriend arrived and seen her house burned to the ground she was crying out hysterically because she knew Bingo was up to something when he came to her house at 4 am in the morning carrying a duffle bag full of money and drugs, Logan's girlfriend Savanna was able to tell the police who the two dead men were but she really didn't know what happen while she was gone but she did know it was something that Bingo started, she was very upset not only did they burned her house down with everything she owned but the money and drugs Bingo had was also gone, she didn't have nothing left her man was dead and her house was now burned down sitting on a vacant lot.

Savanna was now looking for some place to stay when she looked over to her left and seen the garage was still intact she thought at least she could stay there for the night until she came up with a better idea, Savanna was stretched out on some blankets on the floor when she notice the duffle bag sticking out from behind the unused water heater, she jumped up and pulled it from behind the heater and unzipped it when she seen all that money she was smiling from ear to ear because now she could put her life back on track.

King was sitting down in his living room having breakfast when the news came across the screen talking about a big explosion that happen in the area of grant park, king thought to himself that nigga Bingo thought that he was going to get away now look at that stupid ass nigga he done gone and killed himself and somebody else, King started to think if the person that died with Bingo was his cousin Logan that Bingo didn't think he knew about, King just said oh well you reap what you sow and one day he knew he would be doing the same thing reaping what he sow, but right now he wasn't going to be reaping nothing but clocking dollars.

King watched the news until it went off he wanted to make sure he heard the news caster right when he was sure he picked up the phone to call Dallas to let him know what went down, then he told Dallas to pick him up in an hour, King called Skye to see was she up for some company she said sure King took down her address and jumped in the shower an hour later he was headed to sky's apartment where he stayed the rest of the day eating, drinking and making love to Skye.

———————— •●• ————————

chapter nineteen

Smoke Chasing A Dream

———————— •◦• ————————

Cane a.k.a. smoke was really getting fed up with the bull-shit his mother baby girl and King was throwing at him, he felt that they was doing shady shit together and leaving him out the loop, so he decide to get his own crew together, smoke was still in school he had at least six guy's hanging on to him like he was made of gold, smoke had started selling drugs at school only on command he didn't put the word out that he was the man to see, he just made sure just a selective few knew he had the drug's of their choice.

Smoke was on his grind one day after school he was standing in front of the corner store when his uncle king rode up on him, King asked smoke what he was up to when smoke responded by saying I'm just chilling waiting on my home boy, King told smoke come on jump in we need to talk because I heard you generating a lot of trouble around in the hood that we need to settle right now "homie", Smoke said what the hell and got into the car with his uncle.

King asked his nephew what he does on a daily basic when he's not in school, smoke told King why should I tell you what I'm up to when you and my mother do y'all dirt on the low trying to keep me out of the loop that's some bull and you know it, King looked in his nephew eyes and could see the hurt that he was harboring inside so he thought that he could try his hand at a more gentle approach toward getting smoke to open up to him once and for all, smoke was giving King a death stare because in reality he didn't like the fact that king had the drug pin status and his mother was in business with King.

King knew for a fact that his nephew didn't really like him but he was set against making thing's work with him and his nephew for the sake of his sister, so king asked smoke if he would like to hang out with him, Smoke asked king why now what is it that you think that I'm doing that you have to keep tabs on me, King told smoke you my nephew and I love you man and that should be enough don't you think, smoke told King what I think is you should stop treating me like I'm a lame ass nigga like I been dropped on my head or something, I can't believe that you would rather hire outside nigga's to guard your back rather than family what's up with that "huh" King tried to explain to smoke how dangerous his business was and that if one of his soldiers was to get killed in protecting him it wasn't know sweat off his back because they get paid to serve and protect him at all cost.

Smoke understood were his uncle was coming from but he still wanted to be in the game business with him he made sure that King knew exactly where he was coming from as well, he also told king he had a few bodies under his belt ass well he explained to his uncle that he could be his secret weapon that no one had to know about, King was shock to see that his fifteen year old nephew had enough since to know that he was being played by his own family by keeping him out the game, smoke told king to keep it real with you, you started out young yourself and you are only just four years older than me now you tell me what's up player, king went silent because smoke was dead on in what he just said to king but it wasn't about just king it was about his sister as well, she wasn't about to put her baby on the chopping block.

King knew if they didn't adapt smoke in the game with them he could easily be mislead to go the other way against them, so king knew what he was about to do was going to start conflict with him and his sister if she ever found out that king was about to put her son on to the family drug business, king decided to give smoke a trial run so he told smoke I'm going to give you a key of pure uncut cocaine to see how you can handle the pressure of cooking, cutting, and bagging and selling your product and you only have one month to show me what you about if you can show me that you about business I will personally talk to your mother about your performance.

By the time King was finished talking to smoke he was a newfound young man he thought that his uncle was finally on his side for a change, smoke got dropped off back in front of the corner store where king picked him up from, his friend was walking toward the store right when smoke was getting out of the car with his uncle, his friend Chris wanted to know why Smoke was smiling so damn much, Smoke looked at Chris and said we just came up in the drug game nigga so let's go get this shit cracking my nigga, Smoke finally felt like the tables was turning in his favor for a change so he was going to make the best of them.

King was nervous as hell about giving into his nephew wish's he knew once his sister got wind of what he done she was going to chew his ass up and spit him out, king only hope was that his nephew fucked up

the product so he could cancel out his contract before his sister finds
out what he did, but what king didn't recognize about his nephew
he inherited the same gene pool that he had they were both cut
from the same gene pool, so for smoke to fuck up the product was a
understatement smoke was going to make his uncle proud to be his
uncle.

Smoke had been selling drugs for a while he had the game and gone
with it, it was just something that king and his mother didn't notice
because they wasn't paying too much attention to smoke because they
were too caught up in their own lives to see that smoke had already
mapped out his own destiny, Smoke and his friend Chris formed a
small army of soldiers of their own with the four guys that they had
already they recruited four more of the toughest young nigga's they
could fine from the hood, together the eight of them called their
selves the hard eight.

The next day smoke had one of his soldiers crack head aunt to let
them cook and cut their dope in her apartment she was more than
happy to help them cook, cut and bottle their product that way
she could get her free high the whole time she was helping them,
Connie the crack head aunt was about her business when it came to
getting the product where it needed to be, she used to have a drug
dealer boyfriend that taught her the tricks of the trade of cooking
and cutting up cocaine, only thing that Connie hadn't thought about
was these young guys was going to have her ass buck naked dealing
with their product because Smoke was just like king when it came to
business he wasn't about to get taken by no crack head.

Smoke dreams was finally coming to a reality he was getting a chance to show that he could handle the family business now that he had his foot in the door he was happier than rabbit at a Easter egg hunt, smoke was going to show king that he was just as good of a drug pin as he was or even better one. Smoke had already build up his clientele he had so many clients that his little drug house was bursting out the seams, he was happy that he sold the key of cocaine that king gave him in two weeks time, when he took the money back to king he was mesmerized because he had over looked the quality of what his Nephew could do for their business or was he just creating a monster.

chapter twenty

Angel's Return

———— •••• ————

Angel had been gone for two years and six months she was finally ready to get back to her life she had been missing her children and her grandson, she was so happy to be coming out of hiding she also had a surprise for her children she knew that they would be happy to see her plus the element of surprise when they see that she has brought back a very beautiful gift with her, angel and Ramon had been enjoying their lives so much until sex just became a second nature to them they would sleep eat and have sex every day like it was just an excise, Angel knew that she would eventually get pregnant because she wasn't on any kind of birth control so she just speed up the process of getting pregnant because she missed her other children so much.

Angel had a beautiful little girl six months ago name Keiasia she was the spitting image of her son King they both looked just like their mother and father, Ramon was the happiest father alive to have two beautiful children by the woman he loves so much, Angel life has transformed so much since she had been in hiding from the feds she had matured a lot she found out a lot about herself while she was in the Amish community, angel really didn't know if she wanted to continue her life as an assassin or become the best mother she knew she could be, angel had gave it a lot of thought on how she wanted to continue her life as a Columbian assassin she didn't want that life anymore she still had killing in her blood she just thought it was time to retire for a while.

But first Angel wanted to make sure that everything on the home front was fine before she hung up her artillery, plus she hadn't told anyone that she was hanging up her guns yet she was still contemplating rather or not she was fully ready to retire, she hadn't been in the real world for a while and she don't know what had changed since she's been gone but she did realize that she has completely changed, she just hope that her children has kept things in order while she was gone she didn't want to have to come back to them the way that she was, but if she needs to, there will be hell to pay if she has to step back in her assassin mode.

Angel and Ramon with their new addition to the family rode all night they were headed to angel's condo on the out skirts of Chicago, Angel was going to be in for a surprise herself king had totally changed the condo to the style that he liked without informing angel that he even took over her property, when Angel and Ramon finally made it to the condo king was at king towers so he didn't even know that his parents were in town, Angel wasn't angry at all when she arrived at her condo because she wasn't planning on staying in the Chicago area she was only stopping by to make sure everyone was alright before she moved on.

Angel had purchase a burned out cell phone on her way home she was going to call her daughter to have her meet her somewhere close to her condo, when she dialed baby girl's cell number she was talking in codes so her daughter would know who she was, when baby girl seen this strange number come up on her phone she knew right away that it was her mother.

Baby girl didn't pay close attention to the clicking sound that was going on with her phone the feds made sure to keep her phone tapped so that one day their lead would lead to a positive one, and their hunch was right angel surfaced at the right time for them she was about to have a shoot out with the feds and she didn't know it, angel had baby girl in her arms hugging her when she heard a lot of tires coming to a screeching sound outside the empty building they were standing in, she turned just in time to here one of the officers say come out with your hands up are we will shoot, they didn't know angel had an underground tunnel to get away if she needed to escape, but before her and her daughter could stop hugging each other to run into the tunnel the first shot came ringing through the window ripping the walls to shreds behind them, angel got hit once in the leg before she got pissed and returned fire, she had always stayed prepared for anything and at that very moment is when she started shooting nonstop until both of her guns were empty, she didn't expect for the feds to be still following her daughter but she did know that they wanted her ass on the chopping block.

Angel had two guns with such heavy piercing bullets that she killed two FBI agents she tore into their bullet proof vest ripping them suckers into, she did wind up making it to the tunnel only to be carried the rest of the way by her daughter baby girl, Angel's leg was bleeding furiously baby girl had to take her scarf off her neck to tie around her mother's leg to slow down the bleeding.

The feds wanted angel so bad they could taste her blood not only had she been from state to state on killing sprees but she had the nerves to show back up in Chicago like she wasn't wanted, the feds really didn't think that angel had escaped out of the building she was in because they were still shooting up the building they even went as far as throwing in smoke bombs trying to get her to come out.

Angel and baby girl made it back to angel's condo when she arrived Ramon was already on the phone making arrangements for their mafia doctor to fly to Chicago to take care of angels leg, baby girl had put in a call to Ramon letting him know what happen with the feds and that her mother had been hit in her right leg, baby girl had seen some crazy shit spending time with her mother she seen once were she had been drugged up beaten and raped now this, she herself needed to make some changes in her life as well she was finally getting in touch with her emotionally side something she never had the chance to feel she always ran off of action rather than physical pain or emotions.

The mafia doctor finally arrived to take care of angel's leg he told baby girl and Ramon that if the bullet had of traveled two inches more angels would have lost her leg, the doctor fixed up angels leg and gave her enough morphine to keep her knocked out for a while so she wouldn't have to deal with the pain, while angel was asleep she was in deep thought about her life for the first time in her life she was frustrated with the turn of events of her life, she was beginning to feel what her daughter was feeling emotions, she had to find away to turn her life around if not for herself than for her children she started to dream about how all of the madness started with her life in the first place.

Angel thought back to the time when she got out of college she was happy then she went to college to become a criminologist and she past ever test that she took, she had good friends and a family life she had a well rounded life, so the question to her now is how did she really turn out to be a killer with so much bad animosity, she went back in time while she was sleep to uncover her life history to see where she failed and how did she get to this point in her life.

Angel thought that all of her failings had to come from genetics it's something she missing she has to determine what's next in her life does she want to continue on this path of destruction or does she want to try her hand at a more productive life, but first she thought she has to find out what made her take the road to destruction in the first place, she knew for sure that her life started off great she had a nice family two twin brothers, a mother and grandfather that loved her very much she thought, until one day she was hit with the fact that the Salvador's wasn't who she thought they were, angel realized that her whole life had been nothing but lie's right at that very moment angel started to flashback on the time when she first remembered her mother saying to her that she might be a little girl right now but one day she would grow up and realize that the world doesn't old you anything in order for you to prosper in life you have to make things work for yourself, angel didn't know at the time but right after her mother told her that while putting her to bed that night was going to be the last time she would ever hear her mother speak again, angel did remember a lot while she was drugged up on the morphine everything was manifesting in her head about how she got so turned around in her life it really started when she was five years old when she got molested by her uncle.

Cane and Gloria was always on a paper chase leaving his brother Cameron to look after angel neither one of them noticed how she used to react every time they would pull up to Cameron's house, she would be screaming at first and then all of a sudden she would become very withdrawn Gloria trusted him because her husband Cane vouched for him because he was family, little did they know he was a undercover child molester.

Angel's life had took a beaten at an early age yes she was born a normal little girl but with the parents that she had wasn't anything normal about what she was about to face, angel was tossing and turning the whole time she was knocked out from the morphine she was having flashbacks after flashback, she had blocked out a lot of things that she didn't want to remember but in order for her to move forward she had to face her demons, she didn't remember to much about her father all she could remember was when he would play with her sometimes and carry her on his shoulders he would always call her his baby girl, her mother on the other hand would put her in school pull her out of class without warning it was like she was always running from something and she was too young to really understand what was going on, angel also seen the scene unfold right before eyes of two men coming to her house late one night because she knew that her mother would always put her to bed on school nights at eight.

The two men she saw one she would call Uncle Tony the other one she didn't know but she knew something was wrong because she could hear her mother screaming and furniture being pushed around, so angel being the child that she was she got up out of bed to see what was going on, when she seen her uncle and this other man standing there with her mother around the neck she ran into her uncle with full force trying to get him to leave her mother alone, killer grabbed angel and told Tony to handle his business killer took angel back to her bedroom where he put her to sleep with a little chloroform.

Angel never knew how her mother really died she just knew it had something to do with her uncle Tony and this man she knew as killer, what killer didn't know while him and the driver was on their way back to the Salvador's angel had woke up in the backseat of the car and heard everything that was being said between the two of them but she was still drossy and couldn't understand what was going on, this was the third thing that had entered her life and tore it apart, she was only seven years old and her young life had been turned upside down, she started wiggling a lot trying to confront the demons that was hunting her thoughts it was time for her to put her past behind her and move forward.

When angel finally woke up from her morphine induced sleep she had come to terms with all the bad things she had been through in her life she even felt bad about all the pain and suffering she caused other people by killing their loved ones, what she didn't have was bad feelings about killing the Salvador's because they killed her parents and lied to her about being her family and in reality they knew she wasn't a part of their family they were the ones to destroy her family.

Angels last thought was to become something no one ever showed her until she was with the Amish community that is to become a mother to her children and to change her life style, angel looked different to Ramon she looked like she had been to another planet or something because she had a glow on her face that showed him that she wasn't that killer assassin anymore and that he had finally seen what he wanted so much for her to be his wife and mother of their children.

chapter twenty one

Kings Sidekick Skye

—•—

King thought by just kicking it with Skye for that one night that it was going to be just sex and he would move on, but with Skye it was more to it than him just sleeping with her she had a agenda and she wasn't going to just let him slip out of her hold so quickly, king was her way into the inside she wanted to get close to his sister so she wasn't going to let him out of her grip so soon, she wanted his ass on her side so he was either going to play by her rules or she was going to tell his baby momma that he was playing house with her, Skye had made up her mine about king yes he was fine as hell and he had the sex game on lock but she wasn't in it to win his affection or his love she was trying to win back her man Brooklyn from king sister baby girl.

Skye was so twisted in the head until she haven't even realize that baby girl and Brooklyn was just beginning a relationship, Brooklyn was stilling wondering how he ever met Skye in the first place, king happen to be on his way to club sexy when he got a call from Skye he didn't recognize the number but he answered any way, he answered with "who this" and Skye asked him why did he talk like that he said Skye she said yes, king said how did you get my number she told him while he was sleep in her bed she got his phone and called her phone and his number showed up on her caller ID, king look at his cell phone while she was still talking he said to himself this bitch is crazy for "sho " he told Skye look Skye you knew I was involved with someone when we met I told you that you couldn't call my phone and now you trying to stir up some trouble.

Skye had to think of something quick so she told king she think she might be pregnant king told her if you are that baby don't belong to me, she said why not, king told Skye don't be stupid "ma" I might be young but stupid is not in my genetics, she said you know what king fuck you with your arrogant ass you know this your baby now you want to play like your sperm is not potent, you know what Skye you just a educated stank hoe and I don't need this shit so if you like living I suggest you move on with that bull-shit, Skye was so pissed that king played her like a used pinto that she started screaming all kinds of obscenities in his ear, king said listen Skye hear me and hear me good if you ever come around me again with all that noise you talking you are going to be missing in action and baby girl that's real talk "you feel me " before king could say anything else Skye said I wonder how your little girlfriend would feel knowing that you sleeping around on her having unprotected sex.

King pulled into the parking lot of club sex and threw his hummer in parked and before he could say anything he held his finger up to Dallas and Detroit to be quite, he put his phone on speaker so they could hear how stupid Skye ass was she screamed into the phone don't get quite now you stupid ass punk you messing with the big league now I'm show you what time it is young blood, I'm a seasoned woman I'm not no young bitch you went and snatched off some street corner, you should know that I'm going to make sure that you don't go make any more sperm deposits nowhere else without letting little miss sunshine know that her man is out here in the streets fucking women in the raw.

King hung up on Skye he didn't want to hear nothing else that crazy deranged bitch had to say, Dallas and Detroit looked at king like he had stuck his foot in some shit because just because it look good to you doesn't mean that it's good for you, that was something they mention to king when he ran into Skye at the mall, Dallas said not trying to be in your business young blood but everything that glitter isn't gold.

King had really made enemies' with Skye she was angry as hell because she had lost her only way to get inside to info trade baby girl's world, she knew she had to come up with another way in, so she said to herself I think I should become friends with little miss sunshine, Skye knew that Aphrodite worked at the dentist office as a receptionist so she made an appointment to get her teeth clean, she had set up an appointment for two days later which would be that Friday after noon at 12: o clock.

King thought back to the day he met Skye he said to himself I can't believe that I didn't know that bitch Skye was psychotic, that lets you know that every pretty face you see isn't always just pretty it's something hiding behind those eyes, king was always taught that the eyes were the window to the soul but he was so taken by her beautiful smile that he didn't pay attention to her eyes.

King kissed Aphrodite on her way to work that Friday morning he had no idea that his world was about to crumble because he couldn't keep his soldier in his pants, one thing that young king was going to find out was a woman scorned is your worst kind of enemy, king should have known better to step out of character messing around in a cougars back yard now he's going to find out how it really feels to have your ball's pulled tight in a vise grip hold.

Skye hadn't took her medicine in two days she was hearing voices again she was schizophrenic she suffered with this mental illness since she was sixteen, when she first got diagnosis she couldn't understand why her but she found out later that she inherited it from her mother, Skye had become very delusional and she started hallucinating Skye was so messed up until she thought that she would see Brooklyn walking down the street with baby girl or she would see them sitting in a coffee shop drinking coffee, she knew she needed her refill of medicine three days ago but she got tired of depending on her medicine to make her feel a certain way.

Skye had an hour before her appointment at the dentist office she had to pull herself together long enough to befriend Aphrodite, once she arrived inside the dentist office she couldn't believe her eyes Aphrodite resemble her a lot that's why her so-called man was drawn to her, Skye said to herself I'm going to be the best friend she ever had, once I gain her trust I'm going to kidnap her so her young stud of a man can come and rescue her, that way I could get him to bring his sister to me in exchange for his woman and child, Aphrodite signed Skye in for her appointment she even took her vitals to make sure her blood pressure wasn't up, Aphrodite did realize that Skye was staring at her a lot and it made her feel very uncomfortable so she finished up Skye's vitals and left the room.

Skye knew she might have made Aphrodite feel uncomfortable so she decided to apologize to her before she left the dentist office, she came up with the idea to tell Aphrodite that she reminded her of her dead twin sister and that she was so sorry for staring at her like she did, Aphrodite asked Skye what happen to her twin and she broke down crying trying to get sympathy from Aphrodite and it worked she was hovering over Skye like she told her she had just been diagnosis with cancer or something.

Aphrodite decided she was getting hungry so she asked Skye if she wanted to go across the street with her to have lunch and Skye accepted, Aphrodite felt sorry for Skye so she thought maybe she could get her mine off her troubles for a while, Skye told Aphrodite that her twin sister was on her way home from school when she was kidnapped by a man in a blue van, the man was waiting in the van when her sister walked by his van he jumped out threw a pillow case over her head tied a rope around the pillow case and hit her upside the head knocking her out cold, her sister was missing for six months when they finally found her sister again she was face down in the river with her throat split, she had been raped and beaten to death and left in the river dead like a dog.

Aphrodite had to get back to work so she told Skye that if she ever need to talk she could call her, Aphrodite gave Skye her phone number so she could stay in touch not knowing that Skye was crazy as all get out, once Aphrodite left the restaurant Skye was sitting there smiling like the joker in the movie bat man, because she had just set her knew plan in motion.

King was going to regret meeting Skye or should I say she's going to regret meeting the Carter family.

chapter twenty two
Angels Baby Daughter Keiasia

————————•●•————————

Angel hadn't even had a chance to introduce baby girl and king to their new addition to the family, when baby girl finally got her mother back to her condo after the shot out with the feds she was surprise to hear a baby crying in the other room, she walked toward the bedroom to see Ramon sitting there in a rocking chair with this pretty little curly hair little baby, she asked Ramon who baby was she because she is so beautiful, Ramon told baby girl this is your little sister her name is Keiasia Deanna Carter, baby girl couldn't believe her mother had another child and she hadn't told her she has a baby sister.

Baby girl was bursting with excitement she was happy she had a little sister she asked Ramon if she could hold her and he said of course you can she's your sister, baby girl held on to her little sister like her life depended on it she was a spitting image of her and her mother she even had those big beautiful hazel brown eyes like angels, baby girl looked in her sisters eyes and started to pray that their family history had to change for the better for her sisters sake, their mother has to realize by now that she can't keep her children in that same old life style that they were still living in.

Gloria (baby girl) thought it was time to have a heart to heart with her mother about the changes she needed to make, she had another child now that she need to think about she needed to grow up with both her parents and in a more productive environment, baby girl knew it wasn't any hope for her and king because they were in the drug game to deep, but her mother was now forty three years old now it was time for her to settle down and make a life for herself and her sister without all the unnecessary baggage that comes along with being an assassin.

Baby girl didn't have a clue that her mother was two steps ahead of her angel mine was made up the moment she woke up from her induced morphine sleep, she had already discussed with Ramon that she wanted to leave Chicago as soon as she was able to leave she didn't want her daughter keiasia growing up to none of the madness she had subjected her other children to, angel wanted to start over somewhere else and in a environment where she didn't have to watch her back and carry guns in her purse like she was doing now.

Angel wanted Keiasia's life to be fulfilled with happiness and joy she wants her daughter to go off to college and become the best she could be at whatever she wanted to be, she didn't want her daughter to be motherless like she had been she knows if she don't get her life turned in the right direction her daughter would be in the same messed up generation gap that she was in, angel asked baby girl to get in touch with king so she could talk to the both of them together she even wanted to see her grandson little Cane, angel had been out the loop so long that little Cane now known as smoke is in the family business deeper than her and her daughter baby girl knows, baby girl called king and told him she was at the condo and he needed to get there fast, he asked was everything alright and she told him no and that she needed him at the condo immediately king didn't like the sound of his sisters voice so he rushed to get back to his condo.

King arrived at his condo in twenty minutes flat he didn't like his sister sounding so sad he thought something had happen to her the reason why she sounded like she had just lost her best friend, when king put his key in the door to turn the lock to unlock the door but before he could open it, it flew open with his father standing there holding a baby he was so happy to see his father he knew his mother was somewhere close all he could do was grab his father in his arms and cry, king stepped inside and saw his sister sitting there next to his mother on the sofa he ran to his mother and broke down crying again only this time it was none stop.

Angel grabbed her son by his chin and kissed him on the cheek because in her eyes king was still her little baby boy, king realized that his father was still holding this baby so he asked the same question his sister asked who baby was she, angel said king I want you to met your little sister Keiasia she's six months old and we all need to talk about the changes that's going to take place, king asked to hold his little sister he sat down next to his mother on the sofa looking into his little sister eyes, he could see the glow on his mothers face it looked like she had totally changed, he looked at her leg and it was bleeding through the bandages she had on her leg king asked her what happen and she told him it didn't matter because she had a wakeup call that will change her life forever.

King was so angry he jumped up and said out loud to everyone that was in the room it does matter who ever did this to you will pay with his life and that's my word, angel said son you have to understand that what happen to me was called upon me for something I decided to do it wasn't anyone's fault you reap what you sow and it was just my time, king couldn't understand where his mother was coming from it was like she had stepped out of her body and into someone else's, angel told baby girl and king that it was time for her to retire she had to get her life in order to keep from getting killed or going to jail for the rest of her life, she also told them that none of them ever lived a normal life and it was time that they clean house and start with a clean slate.

King told his parents that he loved them but he didn't want to leave what he had his life was comfortable to him the way it was, angel tried to plead with king because she didn't want to have to bury her child, baby girl was on the same page as king angel sat them up in a world of crime now that she was changing her life style she wanted them to do the same but the wasn't having it, the life of crime was the only thing they knew from as long as they could remember, angel said you know what you guys are right just remember that I love both of you and if you ever need me I will be here, but I will be leaving Chicago as soon as the doctor tell me I can travel I will be rooted somewhere I know I can survive without killing everyone I come in contact with, king my son I hear that you are going to become a father in a few months is that true, if so you need to be getting yourself in order as well you don't need to leave your child behind without a father.

Angel had really started raining with sympathy she hated herself for not bringing her children up the way she suppose to have done, but it was too late to try to correct her wrong only thing she thought she could do was pray that they would come to their sense's before it was too late because both of her children were now parents their selves, baby girl couldn't get past the thought that now her mother wants to be a mother she never would have guessed that she would live to see this day come, but even thou she didn't like her upbringing she was happy that her little sister had a chance to live a normal life with their mother and not angel Carter the Columbian assassin.

---

chapter twenty three

Darcey And Olympia

———•◦•———

Darcy had gotten so big over the months she had swollen ankles and face had never been so big, she was glowing with excitement every day and Olympia was spoiling her rotten, she had every maternity outfit that a pregnant woman needed, she was due to deliver the baby in four weeks, Douglas was more excited than Darcy and Olympia he had a decorator to come in to do the nursery the baby was already being spoiled and had not even presented herself to the world yet, Darcy had appointment that morning every time she went to the doctor she had gained five pounds, she felt different this morning from the other times she had to go in for her regular checkup, she felt like it was more than one baby in her stomach because it felt real heavy in her abdomen, so she was going to make sure that this time when the doctor did her second ultrasound that he seen it to she knew he couldn't feel what she was feeling but something weird was going on with her body besides her carrying her sisters baby.

When they arrived at the doctor's appointment Olympia and Douglas was sitting there in the room rubbing on Darcy's stomach when the doctor came into the room, he said good morning and took Darcy vitals and turned on the ultrasound machine so he could began his second ultrasound of Darcy's stomach, when he put that cold gooey stuff on her stomach she started to wiggle around a little bit because out of the whole pregnancy that's the only part she hated, when he stated his exam he heard two heart beats than the camera showed two babies everyone started crying especially Darcy.

Because she was happy that her sister was happy she could help her bring not one baby but two into her life, she looked at the situation differently because they would always have each other's company verse's being without each other, the doctor told Darcy that she would have to have the babies in her thirty fifth or thirty seven weeks because she was carrying them very low that why she was having so much pain in her abdomen.

The doctor told Darcy she was having monozygotic twins she said doctor excuse me but will you talk in terms that we understand please, the doctor laughed at them because he knew that didn't have a clue to what he was saying, he said I'm sorry monozygotic means (identical twins) which means these twins have the same chromosomes and similar physical characteristics, they're the same sex and have the same blood type, hair, and eye color.

The doctor was happy to inform them that Darcy was healthy she didn't have any preeclampsia or gestational diabetes, nor did she have any placental problems or fetal growth problems so she should have a pretty go chance of a normal delivery.

The only problems Darcy was having was getting in and out of the tub and she had her sister Olympia to help her do that so she was grateful to her for helping her, she felt reassurance in knowing she had her sister and brother-in law with a staff of doctors and nurses to help with the birth of the babies, even thou she was warned by the doctor that she would be having a cesarean section she was still a little scared, Douglass explained to his wife and Darcy why she had to have a c—section, because in cases of multiples, though, vaginal delivery may not always be possible, the crowed uterus can cause compression of the placenta or umbilical cord of any of the soon—to be born babies doing labor.

Darcy and Olympia was preparing for the birth of the twins they had even picked out names for them as well, Douglas on the other hand had called his mother to let her know that she will be a grandmother in about three weeks she was jumping with joy she told her son that she would be arriving at his home in two weeks she wanted to be there when they showed they're face to the world for the first time, Douglas told his mother to call him when she arrived in South Dakota and he would pick her up from the airport, time was coming and going very quickly Douglas mother had came right on time because Darcy was getting ready to be admitted into the hospital she was having labor pains and Douglas and his wife Olympia couldn't wait to see their son's being born they were nervous as hell but they held their ground.

When they arrived at the hospital the doctor met them at the door ready to deliver those babies, two hours later Darcy gave birth to two five pound baby boys, the twins looked so much alike until Douglas said he was going to have to have numbers cut into their head so they could be recognized, he didn't want anyone calling them twin he wanted his boys known by numbers are their names, Olympia was crying hysterically she was shacking and everything she was so happy with joy until she literally made herself sick.

The next day after the birth of the boys Olympia and Douglas was going back and forward over what the names should be when they both came up with Dante and Demetrius Darcy told them that was a perfect name for them and since she went through so much pain they agreed to name them Dante and Demetrius, when the nurse came in the room with the babies Douglas and his mother held each child in their arms they were talking about how beautiful they were, while Darcy and Olympia talk about paying Angel a visit as soon as the boys was six months old they didn't want to wait any longer before they approached her because she was a constant reminder to why they were still afraid to live their lives. Darcy told her sister that when they were ready to go after Angel this time they had to make sure they were ready, when Olympia looked at Darcy she told her we both know that Angel doesn't have a conscious so we need to put some of the shit she taught us and switch it around to whip her ass with what she showed us that works.

Right when they about to put a plan together Douglas came over to the bed to thank Darcy again for being their surrogate he told her he will always be grateful for what she did, she looked at her brother—in law and told him she did what she did because they were her family and if she had to do it again she will because that's what family does they look out for each other, in reality the only thing that Darcy and Olympia could think about was wiping angel out because in their mind that was the only way the twins could live a healthy and normal life without crazy deranged aunt Angel trying to kill their mother, Now that Olympia and Darcy was on to the next page in their lives angel was first on the list.

chapter twenty four:

Angel Putting Down Roots In The Stl

---·•·---

Angel made up her mind to move to St. Louis she told baby girl and King that she wanted to be somewhere she thought was secluded, she didn't have no idea how living in St. Louis would change her life but she did remember when she was there on one of her assignments she notice how the Arch stood so big and bright, she remember telling herself that she would come back to Missouri to visit the arch and the downtown area, angel knew when she came to St. Louis on her assignment to kill a guy name black that sold drugs on Blackstone and page, she admired the scenery in Missouri she also picked up on how the people moved around like they didn't have a care in the world, for some reason Angel felt free when she came to St. Louis for that little short visit, angel and Ramon had dinner with baby girl and king to explain to them that they would be moving to St. Louis the first thing in the morning and once they got situated they would be in contact with them.

Baby girl was happy to see her mother take a stand for herself she wanted better for her mother and sister that's more than what her mother gave her growing up; angel and Ramon got up the next morning and hit the road going to St. Louis to find a place they could call home, while Ramon was driving angel looked back in the backseat to see her little angel Keiasia sleeping peacefully in her car seat she knew she had to at least try to come to terms with finally becoming a mother to her children, angel had a map of Missouri she wanted to stay in a condo in the central west end area, she wanted to be somewhere she could have secret departments and tunnels built in so if for any reason she wanted to escape she could, but what had angel frantic was if the feds was looking for her in Chicago they would be looking for her in St. Louis as well.

Angel knew in her mind she needed a fresh start but in reality she knew one day she would have to pay for all the killings and wrong doing she had done, but right now she was going to live as much of a peacefully life as she could for her daughter Keiasia, first thing Angel had to do was find a good plastic surgeon in Missouri that could change her appearance one more time that way she would feel more at peace knowing that no one knew her from Adam, angel found a yellow pages to find a couple of plastic surgeons that she wanted to visit to see which one would be good enough for what she wanted done, she found one in St. Peters, one in chesterfield and out on N. Ballas ct. she called and made appointments to see all three doctors only to find out she liked them all but she liked Robert Baldwin the best so he had the job of reconstructing angel's body from head to toe.

Angel met up with Robert Baldwin three days after arriving in St. Louis he gave angel choices on how she wanted to look to take home with her to study her new image, angel told Robert her mind was made up she wanted to have the image of looking like Halle Berry with the short hair style and all she just wanted her eye color to remain the same hazel brown, Robert told Angel that this would take at least four weeks of transforming her body to the way she wanted it, and it would take another additional two weeks for her body to heal, angel didn't mind because her body had been through so much physical pain she could almost handle anything but dying, that was one thing she feared the most, angel did her home work on Robert Baldwin she found out he was he was selected based on peer nomination process within the list of best plastic surgeon in Saint Louis, MO. He came highly selective in his outstanding work so that's all she needed to know that he was highly qualified, before angel could get the ball rolling in her court she had to buy her and her family a condo in the central west end area, she had appointment to meet with the manger about a condo she seen sitting on the corner of N. Taylor Ave, and Washington Ave, angel met with the manger for the condominium on Taylor ave, she loved the two bedroom unit with the fireplace's, she bought it with cash right on the spot the manger looked at angel in shock because no one ever gave him two hundred and sixty thousand dollars in cash flat out.

Angel and Ramon moved into the condo the next day ready start their lives over, plus angel had to set up appoint with Robert Baldwin to get the ball rolling on her plastic surgery operation she didn't have time on her side so she wanted to get things rolling before she got caught up slipping, angel was living a dangerous life and she knew it she knew one day she was either going to be judged by twelve or carried by six and either way she wasn't ready adaptation.

Angel talked to Robert and they both agreed to her coming into his clinic on that following Monday she told Ramon that she would have to stay at the clinic for the four weeks that Robert had given her, Ramon let her know that him and the baby would be fine go do what she needed to do, that night when they went to bed it dawned on Ramon that he also needed to change his appearance as well he was wanted just as much as angel was, not for all the killings that took place but he was also one of the head nigga's in charge of the Columbia mafia.

Ramon told angel I guess I'll wait until he do his magic on you than I'll go let doctor Robert change my look to what do you think? Angel said you are so right because we both are in the same boat we are known criminals with our face's plastered on the most wanted posters probably everywhere, angel admired the fact that Ramon wanted to change his appearance as much as she did they had to keep a low profile no matter where they went they were going to get notice it was just a matter of time.

Monday was only three days away from angel leaving her baby and Ramon alone while she went to the clinic for her plastic surgery, that Sunday afternoon angel was pushing her baby down Taylor avenue in her stroller when she thought she seen a ghost this guy she thought she killed while on a assignment in St. Louis walked straight passed her and said hello while passing by her, she couldn't believe what she saw because she knew for a fact that the building she sat a fire to he was in the building knocked out cold, so she said to herself how could he be still alive, angel turned the stroller around to follow the guy only to find out he stayed in the same building she stayed in only difference was he stayed on the second floor and she stayed on the fourth floor, angel was deep in thought she told herself this can't be a coincident but in the back of her mind she was going to find out why was he still alive, when she took her baby upstairs he was standing downstairs in the hall lobby, she ran up to her floor with her baby to take her to father, she came back downstairs to see this suppose to be dead man still in the hall lobby the funny thing was he didn't look homeless at all, angel knew without a shadow of a doubt the man she killed and burned alive was a homeless man that wasn't supposed to be in that vacant store front hiding under some cardboard boxes.

Angel was down in the lobby trying to strike up a conversation with the man because this man either has to have had a twin brother or he was like a cat with nine lives, as angel was talking with the man she noticed he had burns to his hands and neck area she told the man she wasn't trying to stare at him but can she ask what happen to his hands and neck, he told angel he happen to be at the wrong place at the wrong time when he was caught in a burning building asleep when a murder was taking place, angel almost gave herself away when her eyes got as big as bow dollars, the man escape the fire from the back door he crawled out of the building still on fire he was able to roll around in some grass to put himself out, what angel didn't know was the man really wasn't a homeless man he came from a family that had money, he happen to be coming from the mall one day and got hit in the back of the head with a butt in of a pistol from a guy who was trying to rob him, the blow was so hard that he couldn't remember who he was or where he belonged when he was found by the paramedics and was taken to the hospital for treatment after the fire, that's when he got noticed by a nurse that was married to his brother the family had been looking for him for months before he was burned in that store front building.

Now that he was back where he belonged he was back to normal and living the life he had his own money anyway he was a doctor at ST. Luke's hospital he worked in the field of brain and spine conditions, angel was happy to hear he wasn't dead because he really wasn't supposed to have been in that building, but she did see he had went from being homeless to living the life of riches he was truly blessed in her eyes because she thought she had killed a innocent man.

Once angel finished her conversation with the guy named Antonio Brass that she thought she had killed she went back up to her condo to tell Ramon the whole story about Antonio and how the whole story about him unfolded, angel was more at ease after talking with Antonio because he told her how god save his life and gave him a second chance to life a righteous life.

chapter twenty five

Conner Finding Answers

———— •••• ————

Conner wanted more than anything to find his sister so him and
Royal teamed up together to find the missing piece's to the puzzle,
Conner went as far as going to the library to use the computer to
find information on his father, he even went as far as bring up the
trial on angel and the killing of the Russian mafia, when Conner
put the names and dates in the computer containing the trial he saw
photo's of the whole trial he also seen a picture of his father holding
this little girl wrapped up in a pink blanket with her head sticking
out of the blanket with head full of black curly hair, Conner started
to feel very emotional he never had the privilege to know his father
or feel the warmth of his father's touch as a child, Conner collected
everything he needed off the computer and he left the library he was
so distraught that he couldn't collect his thought's, he knew one thing
for sure and that is before he left Chicago someone was going to tell
him something about what happen to his father.

That evening Royal came by Conner's hotel room to pass on to him
the information she had received from her cousin José line, her cousin
was just like Royal they couldn't hold shit they both talk like they
had diarrhea at the mouth's so being nosey was just like a every day
job for the two of them, Royal found out that St. Louis was angel's
boyfriend at the time of the trial and that he was also the son of a
Hawaiian kingpin name Cane Cantrell Carter, Royal went on to

explain to Conner that Cane ran the whole south side and west side of the Chicago area, he was the biggest drug dealer she had ever seen she went as far to tell Conner the history of Cane and what she was told of how he died, Royal told Conner that Cane had children all up and down the coast he had at least seven or eight children that she knew of but she wasn't sure about the one's up and down the coast, Conner was looking and listening to Royal like her word was bond he didn't know rather to believe her or just branch out on his own to see if he could come up with his own answers, right when Conner was thinking those thought's in his mind Royal hit a nerve when she told him that his father St. Louis had been shot and killed doing a robbery gone bad by someone he knew.

Royal told Conner that she found out who his sister was but she didn't think it was wise for him to come in contact with someone of baby girl's statue, Conner looked at Royal and said excuse me what the hell or you talking about, you told me you found my sister in one breath and you tell me not to get involved with her in your next breath, are you crazy or what, Royal said out loud to Conner no I'm not crazy I'm just trying to keep you out of harm's way the carters are some very dangerous people, and trust me once you cross that line there's no turning back Conner they will eat you up and spit you out, Conner thought long and hard about what Royal was saying, but his inner need to have family was more greater than what Royal was saying to him, Conner couldn't believe that his mother kept him away from his sister he felt he knew why his mother kept him away from his father knowing that he was dealing in heavy drugs, but why his mother felt the need to keep him away from his sister he didn't have the faintest idea.

Conner told Royal he needed to take a walk because his head was clouded with so much information he felt that his mind was absorbing so much information that his brain felt like a sponge, Royal told Conner she wanted to take that walk with him, Conner told Royal no he needed to be alone just to get some fresh air and think, Conner was walking and thinking so hard until he had walked six miles before he realized that he was in front of a park he sat down and his mind drifted off to he had a big sister somewhere in Chicago, while Conner was sitting on the park bench his cell phone started to ring it was his mother Amy, he answered the phone with hello mother how are you? Amy started screaming soon she heard Conner voice because she had been calling him for two weeks and he wouldn't answer her call's, all Amy could do was cry because deep down inside she knew Conner was in Chicago digging up information on his father she just didn't want him to get hurt.

Conner asked his mother why you couldn't tell me anything about my father. Was it because he was a drug dealer and you were on drugs, Conner broke down emotionally while he was on the phone with his mother he needed to know where he came from and his mother knew more than what she lead him to believe and now it was time for her to speak up or forever hold her peace, Conner told his mother you mightiest well tell me the truth because it's only a matter of time before your little lies will be blown up in your face.

Amy thought it was time to tell her son everything he needed to know she knew if she tells Conner the truth she can finally put her demons behind her, but she knew it will only send her son spiraling out of control, Amy took a deep breath and she started telling Conner the whole story of her relationship with St. Louis and Angel, Amy didn't leave not one stone unturned she told Conner what happen from her running away from home to the day she met his father to the day she met Angel, and how Angel kidnapped him when he was a child and tried to sell him to the highest bidder in the Black market ring she was running, Amy went on to tell her son how angel had her soldiers to kidnap and kill her mother because she wouldn't tell angel where Amy was hiding out when she left Chicago after Conner was born.

By the time Amy was done telling her son the history of her life in Chicago he was more confused and hurt because his mother could have prevented all the psychological pain that he was now enduring, Amy knew now that her son knew the truth he was going to be more determine to get to the bottom of what happen to his father and why, he also wanted to find his sister that he just found out about that his mother still didn't admit to him having, it wasn't that Amy didn't admit to Conner having a sister she just doesn't want him to get involve with the Carter clan ever, she knows once Conner opens that door he would regret it the rest of his life, once Conner hung up the phone with his mother he was on his way back to his hotel room to pick up Royal he wanted to find out who his sister was at all cost, Conner knew growing up that he had other siblings out there in the world somewhere he could feel it, he didn't know why he would always have dreams about playing with his sister and brothers.

Conner grew up with his mother she taught him morals, and standards, respect, but he still wasn't where he thought he should be as a young man he needed his father to show him what it took to be a man, he needed the various qualities and characteristics attributed to men such as strength and male sexuality, Conner can't help but know that his mother kept him in a safe and well educated environment, he made good grades and he never felt that he was hanging around people that wasn't trying to something with their lives, but the truth was Conner was missing a big chunk of his life because it was always just him and his mother there was no other family members involved in his life, he couldn't understand why him and his mother were alone in the world until now she was afraid of something and he was going to find out what or who it was that had their life so sheltered.

Royal took Conner to meet baby girl the kick ass attorney not knowing that she was his long lost sister, Royal had a appointment with baby girl about a drug case she had got arrested on, she was holding two ounces of cocaine for her cousin Jane when they got pulled over for running a red light, her cousin was so high off cocaine when she seen the police following them she took the cocaine out her bra and threw it into Royals lap, when the police walked up to the window Royal was trying to stick it in her bra because she knew male officers couldn't search females, the officer didn't have to search Royal she was straight up busted they escorted her and her cousin to jail with a bond of five thousand dollars secure bond, they were bonded out the next day with pending court dates, she hired baby girl the same day as her attorney.

When Royal and Conner stepped into baby girl's law firm he couldn't believe how beautiful it was she had it set up nice, Royal had a 10:30 appointment and they arrived early thinking that she could get in and out not knowing that baby girl had a client in her office already, once baby girl's client came out and left it was Royals time to go plead her case to baby girl, once Conner and Royal went into baby girls office and sat down they both were in an awe it hit them like a ton of bricks, it was as obvious as the nose on their faces baby girl and Conner could have been twins they both looked just like St. Louis, baby girl was stung she couldn't open her mouth at first, she pointed for Royal and Conner to take a seat once they did she found her voice she asked Conner what was his name? Conner told baby girl his name was Conner Stonewell she went on to ask Conner did he live in Chicago.

Conner told her he didn't live in Chicago but he was born on the south side of the Chicago area, baby girl was in shock because he had that Cherokee blood line going on like she did, the only thing about that was Conner had more Cherokee in him than she did but she could feel a strong connection to this young man.

Before Conner and Royal left baby girl office she made a mental note to check this young man history out because something weird was going on and she was about to find out what, Conner couldn't get baby girl out of his head either only difference between the two of them is they had different mothers but when St. Louis made the two of them he broke the mole, they were so much alike all the way down to their eye color.

Baby girl had to contact her mother to find out what was going on this young man look's identical to her she was interrupted by looking at Conner until she forgot about to tell her mother about her brother that's in the military, she really had forgot she had so much going on in her life, but now that she has moved on from Brad, she can tell her mother about Brads brother being her mother's father Cane son, not only has her mother has another brother but now so does she.

Baby girl remembered offering Conner and Royal a glass of water so she could get some finger prints of Connors so that she could have a friend of hers that work in forensic to run his prints, baby girl took the glass and put it in a zip lock bag and rushed it to her friend she wanted to know who this guy was, only thing she had to do now is get some blood from him and run it through forensic with hers, because she could feel something very strong about this young man and it wasn't nothing that frighten her it was something very close nit.

Baby girl wasn't going to rest until the test results came back on Conner she knew his name and that's it she needed more so she put the call in to her mother Angel, angel wasn't surprised at all when she heard the name Conner she knew one day Conner would show up looking for his father, baby girl asked angel not to lie to her she told her mother he looks too much like me mom not to be my brother, angel ran the scenario down to baby girl about Amy and St. Louis and how she kidnapped Conner and tried to sell him in her black market enterprise, baby girl couldn't believe what her mother was saying if she knew Conner was her brother what gave her the gull to do what she did to her brother, even thou she knew her mother was heartless she didn't think that she would go as far as hiding her only family she had left from her father.

Angel even told her daughter that she wanted Conner's mother dead, baby girl told angel to listen to what she was saying how could you say you changed for the better and in the same breath you say you still want my brothers mother dead, before angel could say another word baby girl hung the phone up on her she said to herself that her mother was a hypocrite, baby girl next move was to make amends with her brother Conner she doesn't know what's been going on his life but both of them grew up without the comfort of their father she only knows what her mother told her about him, and she also knows that her father was also her uncle and he turned on her mother at her trial.

Baby girl was going to set up a meeting with Conner so she could tell him everything she knew about her mother and Amy and their father St. Louis.

chapter twenty six

Brooklyn And Baby Girl

— • —

Brooklyn's court day was fast approaching he didn't know that baby girl had turned over so many stones to get his sentence overturned, when he stepped up in the courtroom he was going to be finally released baby girl owe a big favor for this one she called in killer Murdock for Brooklyn's case, killer Murdock was known for his courtroom antics he would show up in the courtrooms and even the judges would panic killer Murdock earned every dime of his attorney fees, when he received the call from baby girl and she quoted him a price he was on the next flight headed to Chicago it's not every day an attorney like Murdock pull in a million dollars on one case.

Brooklyn walked into the courtroom with his head held low he thought that this would be the end of a long nightmare for him until he seen killer Murdock sitting at the defense table beside baby girl, baby girl waited until Brooklyn sat down and she whispered in his ear this an open and shut case you will be going home today boo" when killer Murdock laid out all the evidence the whole room got quite including the judge because Murdock made it seem like Brooklyn was framed for the murder of his mothers husband, but in reality he was still breathing his stepfather wasn't dead Brooklyn just slow him down, when he left out the room his mother finished the job on her husband he had been beaten her for years she just never reported the abuse and she had finally got fed up with being abused by the man she thought that loved her.

Brooklyn watched as Murdock worked his magic in the courtroom it took all of 45 minutes and he was free to go after he got processed out of the system, baby girl on the other hand had enough time to take Murdock back to the airport to catch the next flight headed back to Atlanta he got paid a million dollars just to do 45 minutes of work he was smiling all the way to the bank, one thing for sure Murdock knew he was good at what he did he also had a wife that was the district attorney in Atlanta he had it wrapped up and sewed up in Atlanta, but he would go where ever he was needed but it was going to cost a grip it he took the job.

Baby girl dropped Murdock off and headed back to the courtroom to pick up Brooklyn she was sitting there waiting for him to be released smiling to herself, because she knew her dreams of being with him was now only a mere dream, she said to herself who said dreams don't come true, when Brooklyn came walking out from the back with his property in his hands baby girl knew it was time to take her man home, when they made it out of the court building Brooklyn couldn't waiting until they got in the privacy of her car he grabbed baby girl by her face and kissed her deeply with compassion, when he finally came up for air snake was squirming with a mind of his own Brooklyn had to literally hold him down.

Baby girl didn't want to take Brooklyn to her house because she didn't know if her son smoke was at home from school yet, plus she wasn't ready to introduce Brooklyn to her son unless she was 100 percent sure he was going to be sticking around before she made that kind of introduction, Brooklyn didn't know that baby girl was two steps ahead of him she had bought him a fully furnished condo on the out skirts of Chicago in the same building where her mother had hers, when he asked her where they were going she just looked at Brooklyn and smiled, Brooklyn told her it doesn't even matter because he would follow her anywhere.

Baby girl pulled up to the condo and Brooklyn lit up like a Christmas tree at Christmas time he couldn't believe that she was so generous, he knew baby girl was more for him than the world was against him he had no doubt that he found his soul mate and that they would be together for the rest of their lives, but first Brooklyn knew he had to cleanse his conscious about Skye because she was out there somewhere and he knew if he was in Chicago she wasn't far behind, Brooklyn told baby girl the whole glory story about Skye and how she manipulated him when he first met her he also told baby girl that Skye had been in the psycho ward for two years, she was on medication for being a psychotic for real Brooklyn told baby girl that Skye doesn't take her medicine like she should and when she doesn't take it she becomes a very dangerous person.

Baby girl told Brooklyn about how someone had been stalking her she also told him about the car that had followed her from her home and to her job, Brooklyn knew right off that it was Skye because if she followed him from New York all the way to Chicago she wouldn't have a problem following baby girl around town, he told baby girl that they should put in an order of protection because it wouldn't be long before she came after them, baby girl told Brooklyn she's not afraid of Skye if she wanted to put her life on the line by coming after her then so be it, but she wasn't going to hide from someone that had a mental condition, baby girl did promise Brooklyn that she would put in the order of protection to cover her own ass, but if Skye wanted to play games with the big dogs she better be ready to reap the benefits that comes with the territory.

While baby girl and Brooklyn was in their new condo discussing Skye she was right outside their window listening to every word they said, she said to herself I can't believe this ass-hole telling her that I'm a psycho bitch that needs medication well both of them ass—holes is in for a rude awaking, baby girl got undressed while Brooklyn watched her he was slowly rising to the occasion she turned on the stereo with Teddy Pendergrass playing soft music in the background she was moving her body to the sound of Teddy's voice and Brooklyn was loving every minute of it, before the music could stop playing Brooklyn was kissing baby girl from head to toe he was melting her flesh with his warm breath planting kiss's all over her body, baby girl was moaning and grunting like she hadn't had a man's touch in years she was so in tune with Brooklyn until she couldn't stop herself, she was finally living the dream only this time horse wasn't in the picture it was snake in the flesh, Brooklyn kneeled down and got in between baby girl's legs he lifted one of her legs and he went in for the kill she was dripping her sweet nectar down Brooklyn's chin until he sucked it all up, when Brooklyn was done devouring baby girl juice's she turned him around and repeated the process on him, it was so hot and intense in that room until baby girl thought that she was going to catch a fire.

Before she could gather her thoughts Brooklyn laid her across the bed and he threw both her legs across his shoulders and he went in balls deep, the penetration was so deep you could hear the both of them screaming out in one hell of an orgasm, baby girl was meeting Brooklyn stroke from stroke until he collapsed on top of her she was so drained until she failed asleep right in Brooklyn's arms.

Baby girl was sound asleep when she heard a loud boom Brooklyn jumped up and ran to where he heard the sound it was baby girl's car Skye crazy ass had put a cocktail in baby girl's gas tank, she was spotted by female that was walking her dog by the condo but the woman couldn't give a good description of Skye because she knocked the woman down to the ground while she was running to her car parked on the corner, but it wasn't a doubt in Brooklyn mind that it was Skye because this wasn't the first time he had this kind of in counter with Skye with another female he used to be involved with years ago.

Baby girl called the police and she went the next morning and put in a order of protection she also put in for a restraining order to keep Skye far away from her and Brooklyn before she kills her for blowing up her BMW, Skye was sitting down the street when the police arrived she didn't think that it was Brooklyn who called the police on her because he never did before, he would just run from state to state trying to get away from her but this time was different he put the police in their business and she was going to surly make them pay for the calling the police.

Brooklyn gave the police a good description of Skye he didn't know that Skye had changed the color of her hair, Skye had even changed her car she didn't want to be seen in the same car baby girl and Aphrodite seen her driving, she said if baby girl wanted to play hard ball fine she better have an aluminum bat because that wouldn't bat she carry's will break.

What Skye crazy ass didn't know she had stepped in some shit because now she was messing with angel carter's daughter and it wasn't a contest? Skye decided she was going to sit there as long as baby girl was in the condo with Brooklyn she said this bitch don't know who she dealing with if she think she's going to take my man, no I don't think so her or her family is going to pay for my pain and suffering.

Baby girl got up early the next morning and headed home to make sure smoke was up and ready for school but when she arrived home smoke was nowhere to be found, when baby girl didn't show up at home like she normally do after work smoke got the hell out of dodge he went over to his boys house and went to school from there, even thou he 's not in class to learn anything these days he just goes to keep the tension down with his mother baby girl, baby girl was so busy with Brooklyn she still haven't paid close attention to her son he's been in the family business for months king still haven't told his sister that smoke is selling their drug products quicker than his own soldiers, baby girl did call the school to see if smoke showed up to class and was impressed when the principle told her that smoke hadn't missed not one day since she got him out the last trouble he was in, baby girl was smiling because she thought that her son had really changed she didn't know he was just showing up in class he had even paid this nerd guy to do his homework for him so he was averaging A' straight across the board.

So baby girl was satisfied with his progress for now but only time will tell what Mr. Smoke has been up to.

———————————•●•———————————

chapter twenty seven
Baby Girl And Brooklyn

<hr>

Baby girl and Brooklyn had been spending a lot of time at Brooklyn's condo she would leave work go home and change and check in on smoke and leave for the evening, even thou she knew that her son could take care of himself she never slowed down to pay attention to his well being, smoke was selling drug's for the family he was also dipping into the product without the knowledge of king knowing what he was doing as of yet.

Brooklyn told baby girl that he would let her know whenever he ran into Skye in the streets, one early morning Brooklyn left the condo and hit the trail for a run as he was jogging he kept hearing someone jogging behind him, when he turned around it was Skye running right up behind him she had been stalking Brooklyn and baby girl for some time now she was so obsessed with Brooklyn until she wore the same jogging suit Brooklyn was jogging in she had the exact same one, Brooklyn stop right in his tracks he asked Skye what the hell was she doing there?

She told Brooklyn with this sinister grin on her face it's a free park isn't, Brooklyn was steaming he grabbed Skye by her arm looked her straight in the eyes he said to Skye look here you crazy bitch I left you back in New York why in the hell did you follow me to Chicago, Skye laughed in Brooklyn's face she told Brooklyn I told you when we first met that you my dear wasn't never going to live a normal life again did you think for one minute that I was joking, Brooklyn made a mental note to himself to make sure that the next time he ran into Skye that he would record their conversation and take some pictures of the encounter with his cell phone so that he could have proof that she was stalking him.

Brooklyn ran faster and left Skye far behind she didn't care because she knew exactly where he was going so it didn't matter to her, as soon as Brooklyn made it back to his condo he called baby girl being true to his word he let her know every detail that took place with him and Skye in the park, baby girl told Brooklyn don't worry about it because her crazy ass will be pushing up daisy's if she don't back off, Brooklyn told baby girl that they couldn't do anything about her being in the park because it was a public park but once she brings her crazy ass back around their condo she can be arrested for dishonoring their restraining order.

Baby girl assured Brooklyn that everything was going to be alright and that she would meet up with him after she got off from work he said alright and they hung up, as soon as Brooklyn thought the coast was clear with the Skye situation he went in the bathroom to run the shower he had no idea the whole time he was talking on the phone with baby girl Skye had broke into the condo's back door with her credit card she had jimmied the door open, while Brooklyn was in the shower Skye was in his bedroom soaking a face towel with some chloroform she didn't want to kill Brooklyn she just wanted to sex him up without his permission, when Brooklyn was drying off he bent over to dry off his long legs that's when Skye came from behind the bathroom door with the face towel and a champagne bottle she knew she wasn't a match for Brooklyn by herself so she had to have something besides the chloroform face towel, Skye hit Brooklyn so hard in the back of his head with that champagne bottle he had no choice but to drop to the floor.

Skye didn't realize she hit Brooklyn so hard because he wasn't moving at all so she grabbed his legs and started pulling him toward the bedroom, once Skye got Brooklyn to the bed he started to raise his hand up to his head that's when she jumped on top of him with her chloroform face towel and shoved it over his nose until he passed out again, Skye looked at Brooklyn's naked body sprawled out on his bed and she smiled because in her mind she was about to have sex with her man without his participation that's how crazy Skye was she didn't care if Brooklyn didn't want her she wanted him and that's all she cared about, Skye took her clothes off and she stood naked looking at Brooklyn she grabbed her nipples and started rubbing them in a circular motion while she slow roll her body toward the bed.

Brooklyn was still in la la land he didn't have a clue that Skye was in the process of raping him she had her body position up against Brooklyn's body on the bed she begin by putting her nipples up against Brooklyn's mouth rubbing them around his lips, Skye didn't care if Brooklyn didn't participate in her sexual activity she was going to please herself with the man she fell in love with, Skye mind was on over drive she was thinking in that crazy mind of her about putting the fire department on speed dial because she was about to start a fire, this time in Skye little sex capade she was going to be calling the shots she was in the position she wanted to be in the cow girl position she wanted to ride Brooklyn all the way to heaven, Skye was having a problem trying to get Brooklyn to salute he was out of it so she had to do the best she could with what she had so she road Brooklyn soft until a light pop on in her head, she did what she used to do to Brooklyn when they were together to get him to rise to the occasion she bent down put her warm mouth on Brooklyn penis and she said out loud there it is come to mommy.

When Skye thought she was in heaven riding Brooklyn like she was on one of those bronco bulls she heard the front door open, she could hear footsteps getting closer to the bedroom she jumped off Brooklyn and slid under the bed, Brooklyn looked like he was sleep so baby girl left him still laying there until she could get a quick shower and join him in bed not knowing that her man had been knocked out with chloroform, while baby girl was in the shower Skye grabbed her clothes from under the bed went in the hall and got dressed and she left with a pissed off attitude because she didn't get the chance to satisfy herself one more time with her man even thou he didn't have a clue to what was going on.

Baby girl got out the shower dried off and went straight to the bed where she thought Brooklyn was sleeping until she noticed some blood on the sheet up under his head, she started shacking Brooklyn to wake him up when he wasn't responding she called 911 for an ambulance when they arrived they noticed Brooklyn had a big knot on the back of his head they could also see his eyes were dilated, By the time the paramedics made it to the hospital with Brooklyn he had started to come to a little but he still wasn't able to tell know one what really happen to him, but he did remember getting hit upside the head and that's all, when the doctor started doing blood work on Brooklyn he did find traces of chloroform in his blood, the doctor went back in the room to let Brooklyn and baby girl know what he found in his blood stream the doctor also order some x-rays of Brooklyn's head because he had a nasty bump that might have fractured his skull, baby girl didn't know what to say because she knew it had to do with that crazy ass Skye but what she didn't understand was why was Brooklyn laying naked across the bed, baby girl wanted answers so she decided to let it go for now at least until she found out if Brooklyn was going to be alright first, after Brooklyn came back from having his x—rays done the doctor came back into the room to let Brooklyn know that he did have a small fracture in the back of his head and they wanted to keep him over night in the hospital for observation to keep a close eye on him.

Baby girl was so confused she didn't know what the hell happen from the time she hung up the phone with Brooklyn until now but she was going to find out, that whole scenario had her spook and she didn't get spook easily but that shit there was crazy it made her think it was something out of a Halloween movie, Brooklyn was slowly coming around but he had one hell of a headache plus he kept telling baby girl that his nose was burning she knew what he was experiencing it was one of the side effects to the chloroform.

Baby girl spent the night at the hospital with Brooklyn that night she called her son and told him that she would see him off to school the next morning, baby girl wasn't taking any chances on that crazy ass Skye showing up at the hospital to finish the job, what baby girl didn't know the whole time she was sitting posted up in Brooklyn's hospital room she had been in the room twice dressed up as one of the night nurses on staff, Skye wanted to make sure Brooklyn was alright too plus she wanted to finish what she started, she had finally got him were she wanted him before baby girl came in the door.

The next morning when Brooklyn woke up in the hospital he really couldn't remember why he was there so he started asking baby girl questions she really couldn't answer, but she did tell him when she arrived at the condo he was naked laying across his bed with blood coming out the back of his head, Brooklyn's head hurt like hell but it was clear to him what had happen to him so he started telling baby girl what he knew, baby girl looked at Brooklyn and said this bitch Skye is beginning to be a thorn in my ass if you don't deal with her soon she's going to be a thing of the past because I don't let nothing or no one come in my world and disrupt my way of living, so either she's going to be dealt with soon or she going to be in the morgue with a tag on her toe for real " you feel me".

Brooklyn seen the look baby girl had in her eyes he had no idea he was in mist of a very bad storm that Skye had brewed up, baby girl didn't tell Brooklyn that she had a very shady past and that she was the daughter of a very known criminal that was wanted in damn near every state, but Brooklyn will soon find out that baby girl is more than the woman who caught his eye, she is a she devil in wolf clothing and he will see her in rear form sooner than he thinks.

Skye was back on her stalking patrol as soon as baby girl and Brooklyn left the hospital she rented her a dark color mustang with tinted windows so she wouldn't get spotted by Brooklyn or his she devil baby girl, baby girl had took Brooklyn back to his condo and she put in a call to Dallas to come watch Brooklyn while she was at work, she didn't want Skye to get the ups on him again so to be on the safe side she called for reinforcement, Brooklyn didn't know baby girl called someone to watch him like he was a child because if he knew he would have told her about herself, Brooklyn was in the bedroom when this icky feeling hit him about Skye being on top of him he was in a deep sleep from the chloroform but he could still feel her sucking on his penis and quite as kept he enjoyed it, that's one of his delights he loved when they were together that Skye could suck a golf ball threw a water hose, Brooklyn knew he had to stay on his toes for now on because Skye wasn't to be played with she was as dangerous as they came at least that's what Brooklyn thought he haven't met the carter clan yet.

Baby girl called Brooklyn to see if everything was alright he told her he was find he also told her that he spotted a black hummer sitting down the street and he know damn well Skye couldn't afford a hummer, baby girl broke down and told Brooklyn that it was one of her brothers soldiers that owes her a favor so she asked him to sit outside the condo and report anything that was out of the ordinary, Brooklyn didn't say anything about that little mishap right now but he will let her know later that he didn't need a babysitter, before they hung up with each other Brooklyn told baby girl he loved her and she responded with ditto.

———————————•◉•———————————

chapter twenty eight

Amy Coming To Chicago

·•·

Amy knew the last time she talked to her son Conner he wasn't sounding to good to her on the phone so she decided it was time for her to go to Chicago to confront her demons, when Amy arrived in Chicago she felt a cold breeze come across her face she didn't ever want to return to a place where she left so much unwanted baggage behind, Amy called Conner to let him know she was in Chicago she asked him where he was staying only to find out they were in the same hotel but Conner wasn't there at the time he was down town having lunch with Royal, Conner knew his mother would throw a fit if she seen him with Royal she was a alright girl but wife material she wasn't and he wasn't about to let his mother see him with the town slut, when Conner got off the phone with his mother Royal had this stupid look on her face she wanted to know who he was talking to that made him smile like he had just hit a big jack pot.

Conner knew by his mother being in town that she was going to stir up some old ghost from her past so he needed to think of away to get her to go back home, Amy was sitting in her hotel room debating if she should go to the restaurant where Conner said he was having lunch with a friend she didn't like his tone on the phone it sounded like he was whispering to her to like he didn't want anyone else to know who he was speaking with on the phone and that bothered her, Amy mind was working her brain to death she wanted to get her son out of Chicago quick she didn't want him to get caught up in that madness she knew Angel and her family was capable doing, she knew angel's daughter was her son sister and she knew deep down inside that her son felt the emptiness to belong to a family but she thought she was family enough for him, Amy went down town to where Conner was and when she peeped through the window and seen him sitting at the table with a girl that was have naked she lost it. Amy walked in the restaurant and stood right in front of the table staring at Conner like he had lost his everlasting mind, Conner said mom how did you find me, Amy said Conner lets go get away from that trash before Amy could say another word, Royal said lady I don't know you and if you call me trash again I promise you that I'm going to hit you so hard you won't remember your damn name, Conner knew that his mother was serious about getting him the hell up out of Chicago because she came out of hiding just to get him to come back home, now that Amy was back in Chicago Conner was going to make her help him in his quest to find out what happen to his father he also wanted his mother to stop running from her problems and face them head on, Conner couldn't shack the feeling that the whole time his mother was acting crazy in the restaurant they were being watched but he didn't know by who but it was a real cold feeling in the atmosphere that sent a chill up his spine.

When Amy asked Conner to leave with her Royal told him if you leave with her you can say good-bye to me because I refuse to be disrespected by some weird out old woman, Conner told Royal my mother is not weird and don't you ever disrespect my mother again, Royal looked at Conner with tears in her eyes because she didn't like the way he took up for his mother but didn't have anything to say about his mother calling her trash, because in reality Conner knew his mother spoke the truth about Royal she was trash with a capital T.

Amy and Conner headed back to their hotel where they sat up all night talking about the turn of events that Conner had found out about his father so far, when Conner told his mother that he didn't blame her for how she lived when she was in Chicago but what puzzled Conner so much was the fact that his grandmother didn't care enough about his mother to save her from the streets of Chicago, When Amy told Conner the real reason she ran away from home it shocked the shit out of him he couldn't believe that his mother was getting molested by her own father and her mother let it happen, when Amy told Conner that she had told her mother the truth about what her father was doing to her she slapped her so hard across the face until her nose started bleeding.

Amy told Conner after her mother called her a liar she packed up her clothes and left without even leaving her a good-bye letter because she let her know that she didn't believe her when she told her that her father would come in her room at night and clam on top of her little body like she was a grown woman, that night Amy let out parts of her life that she never discussed with anyone she just thought it was time to cleanse her soul she just didn't think that it still had that much of an impact on her life to make her fall over in her son's arms and cry like a baby, Conner held on to his mother while she was crying he felt all the pain she was feeling he felt so much sympathy for his mother he wanted to kill his grandfather for what he did to his mother, Conner was building up so much animosity against his mothers parents he couldn't believe that his mother turned out to be a great mother with all that she had been through in her life, now he knew why she ran from her problem and why she made sure she protected him the way that she did he would forever be grateful to her for giving him a life that she never had.

Amy and Conner finally fell asleep that morning the both of them was so tired they finally got the chance to let the ghost's out of the closet it made them feel that a burden had been lifted, but it dawned on them that Conner still needed some closure he wanted to meet his sister and he wanted to know what happen to their father, Amy had been following baby girl all while she was attending Spellman she always knew where to find her just in case angel decided to kidnap Conner again she was going to kidnap baby girl in exchange for Conner if angel decided to go that route again, now that Amy has told her son about her low life father she thought it was time for him to know that his grandmother was kidnapped and murdered by Angel his sister's mother, Amy told Conner the whole story about angel and her family she even told Conner that angel killed her whole family including the dogs, she went on to tell her son she wasn't intentionally trying to keep him away from his sister she was just trying to keep him out of harm's way the Carter family is a force to be reckoned with from drug's to murder and if you crossed them they will kill you and everything you love, Conner knew his mother spoke volume because he had been hearing them same stories from Royal she too was afraid of the carters but she kept her distance from them until she ran into trouble with the law.

Amy told her son if he really wanted to contact his sister she wouldn't stand in his way but if baby girl didn't want Conner in her life they would leave Chicago and never return, Conner agreed to what his mother had just said, but he forgot to tell his mother that the day him and Royal was in baby girls office that she knew he had to be her brother because they looked too much alike, Conner told his mother that he was going to give his sister a call to see if she would meet him for lunch, Amy was really afraid but she couldn't show it to Conner because he was trying so hard to be accepted by baby girl, so she let him have his time she wasn't going to stop him but she let him know if he needed her she would be at the hotel, when Conner called baby girl's law firm she answered on the second ring he told her who he was and he invited her to lunch and she accepted.

Baby girl and Conner met up with each other at the coffee shop across the street from her job for a sandwich and a cup of coffee, once baby girl walked in the coffee shop Conner was already waiting on her she stepped in the door looking like a million bucks and Conner was blown away because he thought his sister was sexy as hell but he was taught never to judge a book by its cover he knew up under all that soft exterior that it was a hard core killer on the inside of his sister.

Baby girl started the conversation first she asked Conner who was his mother and did she lived in the Chicago area, Conner answered baby girl questions he told her his mother's name was Amy and she doesn't stay in Chicago anymore, Conner asked baby girl if he could ask her a few questions and she said sure go head I want to know about you

189

just like you want to know about me, so Conner asked her who was her mother and what happen to their father?

Baby girl had already made her mind up not to lie to him she wanted him to know every little detail about their father and his conniving ways, first she told Conner her mother name was angel and then she went on to tell Conner that ST. Louis was a father that neither one of them shouldn't have known, we both are lucky to have been raised by our mothers our father was a drug dealer and he was an backstabbing crook, I'm sorry I had to tell you that but I'm glad I didn't get the chance to meet him my mother told me that whole story of our so—call father.

Conner wasn't alright with what baby girl had told him about his father even thou he knew he sold drugs for a living it was something else she was hiding and he didn't come all the way to Chicago to play games with her, Conner looked across the table at baby girl he said in a low tone of voice isn't your family drug dealers to isn't your mother an Columbian assassin isn't it also true that right this very minute she's on the run from the law, baby girl looked at Conner like he had just bumped his head she said to him in a loud tone first of all you don't know shit about my family no more than what that bitch Royal told you and she don't know shit about us, and for your information that shit you just spit out your mouth will get you a toe tag quick so watch your mouth, Conner told baby girl if it wasn't the truth you wouldn't have gotten so pissed but since you did now I know what's up with you now, baby girl said excuse you Conner said no sweet heart excuse you your family is behind the death of our father I can feel it I might not be able to prove it but you can bet your ass I'm going to prove it one day, before baby girl could say another word Conner said it was nice to meet the other half but now that I know you are a she devil you are the one that I shouldn't have never known good—bye sister until we meet again because we will meet again.

chapter twenty nine

Aphrodite Going Into Labor

———————— •◦• ————————

Aphrodite had been off work on maternity leave for two weeks
she had gotten as big as an house she was at home cleaning up the
kitchen when a burst of warm water came down her legs, she bent
over to rub her leg when she notice she had blood coming down
her legs to so she picked up the phone to call her mother, when her
mother answered she told her what had just happen her mother told
her not to move she was on her way, when Aphrodite hung up with
her mother she put in a call to king only for it to go straight to his
voice mail she left him a brief message letting him know she had went
into labor and she was on her way to the hospital.

King wasn't answering his phone because he was somewhere he
shouldn't have been he was with some hood rat name Crystal
that stayed over in the hood where he had his dope houses, when
Aphrodite couldn't reach king she called Dallas to tell king she was
in the hospital having his child and if he wanted to be a part of the
birth of his son he should be in route to the hospital right now, Dallas
was so excited he jumped out the car he was sitting in outside the
dope house waiting for king he ran up to the door and knocked hard
enough for king to hear him saying come on man your son is being
born right now, king knew he should have answered his phone but he
was too busy trying to get a nut.

Aphrodite was in full blown labor by the time king arrived at the hospital he did make it on time and thirty minutes later king and Aphrodite had an eight pound twenty one inches long baby boy, Aphrodite had so much pain pushing the baby out until she started bleeding internal the doctors got the baby out and had to do immediate hysterectomy on Aphrodite, they had no other choice because Aphrodite was having chronic pain and she was bleeding heavy and they couldn't control the bleeding, while giving Aphrodite the hysterectomy the doctors un covered something that should have been noticed by her gynecologist visits while she was pregnant, the doctor discovered that Aphrodite had cancer of the uterus which caused her chronic bleeding and pain, which cause for the removal of her ovaries and fallopian tubes.

Aphrodite wasn't able to sign papers for this kind of surgery because she was out of it but her mother gave the permission for the doctors to do what needed to be done for her daughter, Aphrodite's mother did have a lot of questions to ask the doctors before they performed the hysterectomy on her daughter, she asked the doctors if her daughter wanted to have more children what alternatives to the hysterectomy will she have? She also wanted to know was there any other procedure that will help her daughter and still leave her uterus intact. And she asks them by removing her daughter's uterus will menopause sit in soon after surgery, the doctor told Aphrodite's mother that if they didn't remove her uterus she would died because the cancer had already spread it to her fallopian tubes, they had no other choice but to remove her uterus and her fallopian tubes immediately, he also told her mother that menopause will set in after surgery and Aphrodite will never be able to have any more children.

Aphrodite went into surgery not knowing what was going to happen to her it was eating her mother up to have to sign those papers for them to give her daughter a hysterectomy that's something she never had to have herself but she rather have her daughter alive than dead, king was sitting in the waiting area stun he didn't know what was going on until Aphrodite's mother explained the whole procedure to him about the hysterectomy and Aphrodite not be able to have any more children after the surgery, after the surgery was over the doctors came in the waiting room to tell Aphrodite's mother everything went well and she would be able to see her daughter as soon as she came out of recovery, he went on to explain the incision they made on Aphrodite's stomach area which were small ones he told her mother that as soon as the anesthesia wears off she would have to sit up on the side of the bed so she won't get constipated and wouldn't have any problems urinating, he also told her they will give her clear fluids and stool softeners.

The doctor told Aphrodite's mother he will talk more about Aphrodite's condition on going home after surgery tomorrow, king, Dallas, and Aphrodite's mother went down to the nursery to visit their son he was happy and rejoicing about his son but he was tore up in the inside about his girl, he thought to himself how were they going to tell his girl she wasn't going to have any more children was she going to be able to handle what they had to tell her about the hysterectomy she just had, while he was in deep thought about Aphrodite the nurse asked him did he want to hold his son he said yes and held on to his son for dear life as he was holding his son he felt his heart strings pulling at him it was the best feeling that a young man being a first time father had ever had and he loved it, that night king spent his time at the hospital with Aphrodite and his son he didn't have nothing more important at the time but his family and that's the way it stayed until Aphrodite and their son went home.

Four days later Aphrodite and the baby were being released from the hospital and king was more than happy to take them home he had the baby nursery at home decorated by his sister and Aphrodite's mother waiting on their arrival, but before Aphrodite could be released from the hospital the doctor had to go over some details about her recovery at home, the doctor had the staff to give them a list of the instructions she need while at home with special instructions to take it easy, they were to call the surgeon if she had any of the following complications, difficulty breathing, fever over a 100 degrees, black, tar—like stools, pain that sharply increases or becomes uncontrollable, wound drainage problems; redness, bleeding or opening at the incision site, a decrease in ability to function (ex: cannot walk to the bathroom, or a change in level to consciousness or ability to wake, or vomiting, or inability tolerate food or drink, her mother did mine the list of do's because she had planned on staying there with her daughter until she was 100 percent back on her feet so it was all gravy because she had feel in love with her first grandchild, plus Aphrodite was her only child as well.

When Aphrodite arrived home she was fine the first day but the second day she was a mess she went into postpartum depression or should I say the baby blues, she simply felt detachment from her baby and she couldn't figure out way, her mother noticed her symptoms and she explained to her daughter what (PPD) was she told her that she went through the same thing with her when she was born, she told her it was a mix of physical, emotional, and behavioral changes that happen in women after giving birth her mother told her in time it will change she told her she will be alright and sometimes it can last up to four weeks.

Aphrodite's mother was on the money in giving her daughter details on postpartum depression because it's really linked to a chemical, social, and psychological changes associated with having a baby, the good news about that is postpartum depression can be treated with medication and counseling, the actual link between this drop and depression is still not clear, but what is known is that the levels of estrogen and progesterone, the female reproductive hormones, increase tenfold during pregnancy, then they drop sharply after delivery.

Aphrodite's mother found every way possible to explain to her daughter what she was feeling by the time she finished schooling her Aphrodite was tired but she understood her symptoms, king was home every night with his family because he was truly worried about Aphrodite being with his son he knew she was depressed, and she wasn't talking very much these day she haven't held their son not once and that scared him a lot too because he didn't understand what she was going through, she was so out of it that she didn't even notice that king name their son what they together had planned on naming him anyway, his name was Phillip Michael Cater which was Aphrodite's fathers first name and kings grandfathers middle name and kings last name so baby Phillip was all good.

———————————————— •●• ————————————————

chapter thirty

Ava And Denise

———————— •◦• ————————

Ava and Denise had been so caught in Keith and Kaylen until they been putting the rest of their life on hold for instant the law firm they hadn't showed up at work for almost a week, baby girl was beginning to worry it wasn't like them to chose pleasure over business it's was something defiantly going on with Ava and Denise, little did baby girl know them young boys had Denise and Ava ass hemmed up they had them so strung out that they didn't know if the sun raised or shined in the mornings, in order for Kaylen and Keith to control baby girls sidekicks they had been lacing their purple haze weed with cocaine them fools stay higher than a kite flying in Jupiter somewhere they didn't know, until one day recently Ava notice the aroma was different she asked Denise did she feel funny after they finished smoking their blunt she said sure do and I feel as high as that airplane passing by.

Ava knew then that Kaylen and Keith were up to some shady dealings Denise had totally lost her conception of what they were doing, Ava told Denise that's it I know what they trying to do to us and we been falling for the bull-shit but today it ends here, Ava thought of turning the tables on them to let it be beneficial to their health because they were trying to get us hook on cocaine without our knowledge that was some crazy shit don't you think, Denise was so out of it while Ava was talking to her she was sitting there with glass marble eyes staring

197

off in space, before Ava could get Denise to respond to what she had just said she hit the floor kicking she was having a seizure something she never had before until now, Ava was so scared she called baby girl so she could call an ambulance and send it to the hotel where her and Denise had been with Kaylen and Keith for the last week, by the time the ambulance arrived at the hotel Denise had came out of the seizure she didn't even remember what happen it was like she blacked out, baby girl arrived at the hotel right behind the ambulance and she was able to make Denise go to the hospital anyway to get checked out just in case.

Once Denise made it to the hospital and they did her blood work the doctor's discovered that she had cocaine in her system, she told the doctors she never did cocaine in her life and that they had to be mistaken the doctor told her that they ran the test twice and there was no mistake she had cocaine in her blood stream, Denise was angry as a booger bear because she never experiment on any kind of hard drugs let lone cocaine, the doctor asked her did she know that she was eight weeks pregnant she said know what you do mean doctor I have had my period every month like clockwork, the doctor went on to explain that she could still have a period and be pregnant because in her case she was defiantly with a child.

Denise knew she had been getting her back cracked on a regular by kaylen so it was defiantly a possibility, but what was she going to do because she wasn't trying to have a baby by someone who had been drugging her, all she could do was break down and cry because she has messed up she thought she was safe having unprotected sex with him, she knew better but she let him talk her into having sex without a rubber he was talking shit about it don't feel the same, Denise told baby girl and Ava that she can't have that baby, baby girl told her yes she can it don't have anything to do with the baby the baby is a miracle from god it's not the babies fault that she was careless, baby girl reminded her of the situation with her she told her don't forget what happen to me, my son came from me being raped not only by one man but three remember, when Denise thought back to how baby girl was laying up in that bed with two broken jaws and her teeth knocked out she considered herself lucky.

Ava knew she also could be pregnant because she hadn't had her period either but it didn't dawn on her until the doctor came back in the room with Denise's results, so she decided to go in as a walk—in at the peoples clinic the next day she wasn't going to wait she had to know because her body was already changing, after Denise had got checked out the doctor though that it would be good if she stayed in the hospital overnight for observation to run more test to make sure the baby was doing fine, she agreed because she had been so tired lately now she know why she was eight weeks pregnant and she had been drinking and smoking weed, baby girl and Ava left the hospital after Denise went to sleep kissing her on the forehead letting her know they would be back up to the hospital to pick her up in the morning.

The next following morning Ava was at the health clinic before they opened the door she was parked outside sitting in her car she wanted to be the first one the doctor see's when he arrived there, Ava had a little wait because the doctor didn't get to the clinic until 8:30 when he arrived she was the first one the nurse called she had her vitals done weight, blood pressure and urine test done so the only thing she was waiting on was her exam and right when she was taking off her clothes the doctor knocked on the door he introduced himself and the exam was next, the doctor asked Ava when was her last menstrual period she said about three months ago he said ummm . . . she said what does that mean he look at Ava and told her to get dressed once she was dressed he would come back in the room to talk with her about his findings, Ava was scared to death she didn't know what to think because the doctor left her wondering, when the doctor came back in the room with the blood work and urine test he was able to tell Ava she was twelve weeks pregnant and she had cocaine in her system as well and if she was planning on have her child that she needed to be in a treatment center.

Ava was pissed at how the doctor was talking to her but she over looked it because now that she knew for sure she was pregnant her and Denise was rocking in the same boat, the only difference between the two of them was Ava wanted her child and Denise didn't so whatever procedures she had to take she was damn well going to do them to make sure her child was healthy, the next morning baby girl and Ava met up to go pick Denise up from the hospital she was feeling much better than she did when they left her that night she still didn't know if she wanted to keep her baby or not and the doctor told her she didn't have that much time to make up her mind.

While all of them were riding back from the hospital baby girl asked Denise had she made her mind up as far as having the baby she told baby girl she really didn't know, right before baby girl could ask Denise another question Ava busted out and said well I'm having my baby rather you have yours or not, baby girl and Denise was took by surprise because Ava hadn't told them that she might be pregnant too, baby girl threw her car in park she was sitting right in the middle of the street stopping traffic at a green light she was shocked that her friends was so careless and out with these guys that they really didn't know screwing them in the raw, Ava started screaming at baby girl to get her car out the street she was sitting there staring at them like they were stupid because she thought that they knew better, she told them you two stupid crazy bitches been missing in action for two weeks instead of doing something positive y'all out signing death certificates unbelievable.

Baby girl said alright what's done is done now how you two want to handle your babies daddies because in my eyes that was some foul shit they did to the both of you, so it's up to you because if it was me I would go straight up their asses blazing, because it has to be some kind of agenda for them to drug y'all up I mean I don't know what y'all think? Ava and Denise wanted them to explain what was they thinking to put cocaine in their system's like they did was they trying to turn them into zombies or what or was they trying to control them with drugs, so they could flip sides they should know by now if they go up against the carter family all of them will die including their unborn children.

Ava told Denise one thing for sure is I'm going to get some answers or my baby's father will be dead before morning and that's real talk, Denise told her I'm with you it's either now or never and I think we should go find out right now let's go girlfriend, and they both headed out to the hotel where their expected fathers were staying, baby girl wished them good luck and told them if they needed her she was only a phone call away.

---

chapter thirty one
King Pampering His Little Shorty

—•—

King was so happy being a father he was buying baby clothes like crazy in one day he spent over a thousand dollars buying baby clothes, he was so excited he had forgot to call his parents about their new grandchild Phillip he had pictures on his cell phone of his son so he called his mother to let her know that he would be sending her a surprise over the phone, angel knew from the tone of her son's voice that he was excited about something and she hadn't heard anything about Aphrodite having the baby because if she had she would of been sneaking back into Chicago for the birth of her second grandchild, king was still talking to his mother on the phone when the picture of Phillip popped up on her phone she was screaming like someone had broke into their condo, she told king I can't believe you are your sister didn't call me when Aphrodite went into labor, king explained to his mother now that she was back in their life he didn't want to take the risk of her getting caught up with the police again, but he did tell her as soon as the baby was old enough to travel he will bring the baby to his grandmother for a visit.

Angel was angry at first but king had a way of softening her heart so anything he told her would be alright with Angel, before they hung up king spoke with his father and he asked how his little sister was doing his father told him don't worry he had everything under control he made sure to tell king to take care of his grandson until her could bring him to St. Louis for a visit, they said they loved each other and their good—byes and hung up, King was still in the mall shopping the whole time he was talking to his parents, he went into babies r-us when he spotted the most beautiful car seat made by Eddie Bauer he said to himself my son has a car seat but that stroller and car seat is the shit my son is going to have everything my parents gave me and then some.

King bought the stroller and the matching car seat he has bought so much stuff for his son that Dallas had to call his brother Detroit to bring the other hummer just to get the things that king bought for his son back to their house, when king made it home he was in an awe because Aphrodite had finally came out of her depression and was holding their son for the first time she was kissing all over his little fat jaws like crazy, king not only had a new son he had his girl back too he was as happy as a nigga on death row he even made promises to god that he would change if his girl would come back to her senses and she did so only time will tell if he meant what he said.

Aphrodite's mother was sleep when king came home but she thought she had the baby in the bed with her until her phone started ringing and she noticed the baby was gone she had no idea that her daughter had came in the room and got the baby, when she seen her holding him for the first time she was excited just like king to know that she had over came her depression it was a happy reunion for all of them, that night Aphrodite and king sat up in their bedroom with the their baby laying in their bed between the both of them they couldn't stop smiling at the miracle god had blessed them with.

Aphrodite was back to her normal self and they were back to living
their lives she was enjoying being the mother she knew she could be
her first lesson of motherhood was waking up for the 2 am feedings
she had been missing, her mother had took over being mother and
grandmother while her daughter was depressed, Aphrodite had missed
four weeks of her baby life but now that she was back she was willing
to do whatever she had to do to gain the status of motherhood, she
looked in her baby eyes with all the love she had in her heart she
never knew she could bond with her child as fast as she did now
that she has that motherly love she don't want to leave her son for
not one minute, Aphrodite would carry her son every where she
went in the house if she would go take a bath she would take Phillip
with her in his car seat which would frighten her mother and king
to death, because they thought she would drown her own child she
had became very obsessed with the baby they could be sitting there
holding him and she would come snatch him out of their arms, king
started talking to Aphrodite mother about her behavior he said don't
you think it's strange that she doesn't want us to have anything to do
with the baby, she told king no not at all because she's clamping on to
him because she knows she's never going to be able to have another
child, so she thinks by her smothering him she can prevent what she
is now feeling emotionally that's all give her time king and trust me
everything will be back to normal shortly.

King understood what Aphrodite's mother was saying but that didn't
mean he wasn't keeping his eyes on his son because even thou he
somewhat understood he still didn't trust the fact that she was missing
in action for four weeks before she snapped out of it, king went into
the kitchen to get him a beer when he heard singing coming out of

the nursery he peeped in the crack of the door to see Aphrodite breast feeding the baby, he was shocked because he had never experience a woman breast feeding a baby in real life he only seen it done on t.v. but up close and personal was a first for him and he was thrilled to see his son latch on to his mothers breast like he used to do before she had him.

King and Aphrodite had an appointment in two weeks to take the baby to the doctor for a checkup and king was more amped up than Aphrodite he wanted to see if his son had gained anymore weight, plus Phillip was born with the prettiest grey eyes and cold black curly hair, king wanted to ask the doctor about the strange behavior that Aphrodite was experiencing also because to him her behavior wasn't normal and he wanted some answers from a real doctor instead of her mother that didn't have an degree in anything but drinking on special occasions.

King found out what Aphrodite was experiencing was actually what her mother had told him before hand, she had been prescribed medication for her behavior she just decided not to take it anymore she didn't want to rely on taking drugs of any sorts, when king left the doctor's office he felt much better after the doctor explained the situation to him he was able to breathe a little lighter at nights but he still wasn't going to trust Aphrodite alone with their son for the time being, so her mother staying there with them for a while was more than a notion for king he wanted her to stay there as long as her daughter needed her and for the protection for his son when he wasn't around.

chapter thirty two

Skye Car Accident

—•—

Skye was still running around acting ratchet she was still in front of Brooklyn's condo stalking him and baby girl's every move until one night she got spotted by Brooklyn's nosey neighbor Miss Walters who stayed in the same building as Brooklyn on the first floor, she had been seeing this same car with out of town plates sitting on the corner of their block for a while so she decided enough was enough and she called the police to let them know that an unmarked car has been sitting outside on the corner for days with out of town plates with tinted windows and she thought that it was very odd, she also told them when Brooklyn would leave a young lady would be peeping around in his windows, Miss Walters let them know that if they wanted to catch her they needed to come now while she was on her way back to the car sitting on the corner with the out of town plates, the dispatcher let every officer in the area of 2712 berry lane drive to approach with caution the person they were looking for was sitting on the corner in a black mustang with tinted windows and out of town plates, when Skye heard the police sirens she started to panic because they were getting close to where she was sitting in her car, one of the officers pulled up on the side of Skye and asked her to turn the car off and get out of the car, before the officer could ask her again she speed off down the street two blocks away was the freeway she took a sharp right turn and wind up on the freeway she was speeding so fast going down the freeway like a bat out of hell, she was dodging in and out of lanes going a 100 miles an hour until she was stop by an older gentleman who's car had stopped on the freeway, Skye hit that man's car so hard until it flipped over three times she got thrown through her front window of her car because she wasn't wearing her seatbelt, the accident was so bad until both of them had to be air lifted to the hospital, before they could get the man hooked up to some fluids and oxygen he was already pronounced D.O A. dead on arrival, Skye on the other hand was in bad shape she was in a coma she was rushed to surgery she was in surgery for four hours she had a broken jaw, three broken ribs, and a rupture spleen with a fracture skull so she was tore up pretty bad, the officers that was chasing Skye down the freeway were still at the scene of the accident checking out Skye's car looking for anything she may have had in the car to make her flee from them like she did

They found her purse and pictures of baby girl and Brooklyn and pictures of another young lady that was pregnant they didn't recognize, they only knew of baby girl and Brooklyn because of the restraining order that they had recently put in for her stalking them, the doctors thought it was best that she was in a coma so her body could heal itself, once the officers was done at accident they went up to the hospital to see if they could ask Skye some questions she wasn't able to talk to them and the doctors told the office they doubt if she would be talking to them any time soon, because of the course of the accident her head had been damaged very bad her skull had been fracture in two places so until she woke up out of her coma they wouldn't know what kind of effect it had on her brain as of yet.

The doctor did tell the officers that they could check back in three
to four days maybe she might come around they wasn't sure but
the kind of trauma she sustain to her brain would be a miracle if
she didn't have amnesia, the officers explain to the doctor that she
was wanted for second degree murder of the man on the freeway
and they had to handcuff her to the bed and leave two officers
posted up outside her hospital door, the doctor understood
their procedures and he didn't have much to say as long as they
followed hospital procedures as well.

Skye was in a coma for two weeks when she finally snapped out
of it she when she came to she tried to get up but her hands was
handcuffed to the bed, her mind was clouded she didn't even know
where she was and how she got there she was screaming when the
doctor came into the room to get her to calm down, the doctor told
the officers that was posted up outside Skye door to get out the room
so he could examine his patient, she was hysterical they had to give
her a shot to calm her down she was fighting the doctor and the
nurses, once Skye was given the shot she went out again like a light
switch only to be in a deep sleep again this time she was dreaming
of a baby she didn't have she thought that if she would tell Brooklyn
she had their baby maybe he would give her another chance, when
the nurse entered Skye room and heard her talking to herself and
mention the name Brooklyn twice she knew then that Skye was trying
to pull the wool over their eyes she hadn't lost her damn memory
she wanted them to believe that she had, the nurse didn't feel any
sympathy for Skye because the man she killed on the freeway driving
like a bat out of hell was her grandfather Larry Bishop she wanted
to kill Skye herself, but what she did do was let the doctor and the

officers know that Skye was trying to pull a fast one she remembers who she is and I believe she 's trying to play the crazy card, the nurse told them don't get me wrong I do believe the young lady have issues that concerns me but please don't let her back on the streets.

The detectives that was assigned to the case visited Skye the next day at the hospital they wanted to ask her if she remembered anything about the accident, Skye was trying to play the crazy card as soon as the detectives walked in they already knew what time it was with her they had already been warned, when detective Boil asked Skye why was she running from the police she told him I don't remember running from the police sir, detective Boil looked at Skye with this grim look on his face he said young lady save the drama for the actors their more better at than you.

Skye told detective Boil you know you are one arrogant ass piece of shit and I don't have to answer anything without my attorney present so get the hell out of my room, detective Boil was took by surprise by what had just came out of Skye's mouth she looked totally different she looked just like Linda Blair in the exorcist, Skye looked like a crazy chained up savage her whole demeanor had changed she looked more possessed than anything but not enough to throw detective Boil off his square he knew his job and he has been profiling people for fifteen years so he knew Skye was a damn fool, but he had to give credit where credit was do she had skill's in trying to play them for complete fools.

Skye had been laying up in the hospital for weeks trying to come with a plan to escape and she had to come up with a solution quick because time really wasn't on her side, the doctor had ran some more test's on Skye and found traces of risperidolin her blood stream had been taking medication for schizophrenia, that let the doctors know that she wasn't pretending to be crazy she had some for real issues that needed to be addressed as soon as possible, before she got released from the hospital Skye doctor knew she was going to be released in the custody of the detectives as soon as he said she was free to go but Skye wasn't making it easy for them she was trying to buy some time.

Skye was so busy thinking about Brooklyn and baby girl until she forgot about the hired gun she hired to kill baby girl that was now scoping out his prey, two time Tony was following baby girl around town trying to get the perfect time to put a couple of hot slugs in her but it was hard trying to catch her alone he was told by Skye not to hurt Brooklyn, it was hard trying to catch one without the other one plus two time Tony had no idea that Skye had been in a car accident and was on her way up state for second degree murder, one day in particular two time Tony finally got what he wanted baby girl was coming out of her office going to lunch she was pulling into the parking lot of Dorothy's restaurant and before she could cut the car off and get out Two time Tony jumps in her passenger seat and pull's his gun out and told her to drive off the lot, they were only two blocks down when he told baby girl to stop the car she did what she was told and she asked him what did he want with her, he told her to shut the hell up he was the one to ask the damn questions not her, what two time Tony didn't know was baby girl always stayed strapped so the shit was about to hit the fan, Two time Tony shot baby girl once without warning hitting her in her thigh she bent down to grabbed her thigh and came back up with her 9mm striking Two time

211

Tony in the chest not before he fired off another round striking baby girl in her arm

Two time Tony was deep breathing trying to catch his breath while baby girl was calling for an ambulance for herself she didn't give a damn if two time Tony died for shooting her, but she did want to know who sent him after her, baby girl told two time Tony you might as well tell me because you dying anyway and once the ambulance and police get here you will be dead for real I'm going to killed your ass anyway so spit it out ass-hole you don't have that much time.

Before two times Tony could say anything blood started gushing out his mouth he was trying to tell baby girl that Skye sent him and she's not going to stop coming after her until she's dead.

chapter thirty three

Kaylen And Keith Living In Chicago

———————— •◦• ————————

Kaylen and Keith was living the life in the Chicago area plus they thought they had found them two fools in Ava and Denise little did they know that the girl's was up on their schemes, the sad part about it they wasn't going to tell them since they wanted to play dirty with them they were going to use reverse psychology on them, Kaylen and Keith had no idea they was playing with fire Ava and Denise learned all their treachery from Angel so they knew how to handle a couple of want to be players like the brothers from New Jersey, they wasn't to good in cover up their lies Ava had baby girl to use her skills to find out where they really came from.

Baby girl wanted so bad to kill the two brothers she had already given them a free pass when she introduced them to her brother king knowing they were sent by Buddha's brother Jasper to kill him but she just thought she would keep a close eye on them, Kaylen knew one day that they would have to kill the Carter clan and he tried to get his pig headed brother Keith to realize it too but he was too busy walking around thinking that everything was cool as cool whip, Kaylen had more of a serious demeanor than Keith and they argued a lot about him being so pig headed and not listening and paying attention to the matters at hand.

Ava called Keith to see if he was too busy for company and he ask her why was she planning on coming over she said I was planning on coming over and bring dinner with me if you wasn't busy, he said well that sounds like a plan what time where you coming? Ava told him as soon as you give me the ok I'll be there, he said ok then why you still talking come on over, before she could say anything else Keith had hung up because he was doing what they all did with females use them to his advantage, he had another female name peaches that he had met that day laying up in his bed so he had to get her the hell out of dodge before Ava showed up.

Kaylen was in the other room entertaining his company as well but he was cool he hadn't received a call from Denise saying that she wanted to come over quite as kept she was tired of playing games with him so she decided it was time to cut her ties with Kaylen lying ass, yes she agreed with Ava to teach them a lesson but right now wasn't a good time because she was still wrestling with the fact that she was pregnant, kaylen and Keith had moved into a upscale condo that was two thousand dollars a month on the out skirts of Chicago not too far from the one king was staying in, the two brothers was making money hand over fist because even thou they were now on kings payroll they were still doing conniving shit on the side like selling their own drugs of choice on the other side of town, if king ever found out that they wasn't as loyal to him as he thought they would be floating in the river like the fish's.

Keith had a bad vibe when Ava showed up at their condo she was so antisocial with him so being pig headed he dismissed it, and when they went into the kitchen to sit down to eat the fish and fries she bought for them to eat she started vomiting just from the scent of the fish, Keith was like damn girl what the hell is wrong with you, Ava jumped up and ran to the bathroom she had pulled over about three times already throwing up before she made it to Keith's condo that's why they had to warm the food up when she got there.

Kaylen heard the commotion so he asked his brother was everything alright, Keith said yeah I'm cool all I did was open up the bag with the food in it and she started vomiting all over the floor and shit, neither one of them was paying attention to the kitchen door until they heard Kaylen's company say sounds like somebody is pregnant to me, that's the only time you throw up from crazy ass smell unless maybe she might have the flu who knows that's your company not mines, Keith told Kaylen look get your bitch before I slap the shit out of her for sticking her nose in my business.

Kaylen told Keith don't disrespect my friend she was just informing you of something that you need to take care of because we didn't come here to be any ones damn father we not ready and you know that shit just like I do so go handle that shit for real, Keith really didn't know how to handle asking Ava what was going on with her because he knew what him and Kaylen had been doing to Ava and Denise, so if she was pregnant the baby had to be affected with the cocaine they had been giving the two of them, all of a sudden Keith grew balls and said fuck it I'm going to ask her anyway what can I lose she either tell me or she don't what the hell I could care less, when Ava came out the bathroom the first thing Keith asked her was she alright then he went in for the kill, he asked her what was her

215

problem was she sick with the flu or was she pregnant? Ava looked at him and did what she set out to do she told him yes I'm pregnant what about it you don't give a damn because if you did you wouldn't have put cocaine in the weed I was smoking with your stupid ass, Keith said hold up put the coo coo back in the clock baby because I don't know what the hell you talking about, Ava said oh so you going to keep playing games "huh" alright let me tell you this if you think you are going to keep playing with my emotions then you got another thing coming because as of today the only thing you going to see of mine is my black ass when I turn my back to leave your damn condo brother.

Kaylen came out the kitchen laughing his ass off he asked his brother did I hear her correctly did she say she was pregnant and that you had been lacing her weed with cocaine, Keith said that's what her stupid ass said, Kaylen said ok if she found that shit out I know Denise know as well so what the hell are we going to do know that they are on to us, Keith said we not going to do shit they can't prove it was us so what they think is nothing it's our word against theirs, my theory is this they wanted to hang with the big boys that's what you get when you step in man side shoes, Kaylen told Keith again there you go talking out the side of your next again you knew that shit was foul what we did to them and my dumb ass went along with it, you know I'm not owning up to nothing I'm taking that shit to the grave with me player.

Keith told Kaylen you always been a timid ass nigga I don't know why you came here to Chicago in the first place, Kaylen said to watch your back nigga so you won't wind up with a toe tag you stupid ass nigga, they was arguing so much until they forgot about the Ava situation but they will soon find out that revenge is best served cool.

---

chapter thirty four

Darcy And Olymipa Trying To Find Angel

———————————•◦•———————————

Darcy and Olympia was planning a trip them girl's wanted Angel in a cement grave as soon as possible they were restless and couldn't function knowing Angel was somewhere in the world walking around committing god knows what, Olympia's babies was now six months old now and she thought by her mother-in-law still staying with her and her husband for now it was a good time to travel to Chicago to see if Angel had return or did she back track to Columbia, so their mind was solely on looking up Ava and Denise thinking that they will give them the information they needed it, not knowing that Ava and Denise wasn't going to give them any information to hunt down Angel.

Darcy reminded her sister Olympia did she forget that Ava and Denise was only a pawns in angel's den of destruction, Olympia said you're right but just maybe we can pressure them into telling us by making them think that we were turning ourselves in for the murder of cool, crazy red and his girlfriend so we were going to implicated everyone that was involved, Darcy told her sister I don't think that's a good idea because telling them that will be like signing a death certificate and we both know those to traders is strictly for Angel and baby girl.

Darcy told her sister let's put this scenario together because we were just as much at fault of the killings that we did for Angel as the rest of crew, we can't turn them in without implicating ourselves so that idea of turning them in to the authorities is out so we have to put our heads together to come up with a solution, Darcy had to remind her sister again that we have to make sure when we throw stones that it doesn't land in our house, Olympia said hold up sister girl who talking about throwing stones I'm talking about finding angel at any cost and putting some hot lead to her ass.

Darcy and Olympia thought they were talking amongst each other but Olympia's mother-in-law was ear hustling at the her bedroom door, she heard everything that Darcy and Olympia were saying and she couldn't believe what she heard all she could think about was her son was married to a killer and she was defiantly going to kill someone name Angel, right when Douglas mother was turning around to leave from in front of their bedroom door the floor made a cracking sound letting them know someone was outside the bedroom door, Olympia looked at her sister Darcy she said you know who that was don't you, she said of course I knew who it was there is no one else here but me you and your mother—in-law I wonder did she here what we were talking about, Darcy told her if she did we will know because it will show in the way she acts toward us.

The next following morning Douglas made breakfast for everyone and his mother didn't come down she told Douglas she wasn't feeling very well, so he thought that maybe she was feeling low on her sugar count and took her up a glass of orange juice, when she was about to tell her son what she overheard Darcy and Olympia talking about

Olympia walked into the room shocking her back into reality the look she gave her mother—in-law made her think twice about letting her son know anything about what she heard, Olympia knew for a fact that she was listening to their conversation that day because her persona had changed toward her and her sister you could see the fear in her eyes she was really frighten of her and her sister Darcy.

Darcy told Olympia that they had to do something quick about that situation they didn't want Douglas mother to tell anyone what she heard because if they didn't Olympia could be rising her children from behind bars and before that happens they would have to close Douglas mother's eyes permanently, Olympia was having second thoughts she was caught between a rock and a hard spot she didn't want to kill her children's only grandparent and she didn't want her mother-in—law to send her children's mother to jail either, but what she didn't think about was that she couldn't be charge for the same crime twice it was called double jeopardy, something she hadn't thought about until it popped in Darcy's head and she told her sister they had nothing to worry about plus she couldn't prove anything they could have been discussing a movie for all she knew.

Darcy told Olympia let her tell Douglas as long as you deny her story he won't believe her over you he loves you, so don't worry it will be fine just keep batting those big beautiful eyes and he will fall at your feet like he's been doing trust me sister dear, we both know we haven't had much experience with men but I do know you have what it takes to get what you want, just like Douglas knew what it took to hook you he wore you down until you accepted him as your husband so you guys was united as one when he said I do, Olympia was so happy that her sister was dropping some knowledge on her because her heart was in turmoil she didn't want to lose Douglas she really did love her husband.

Olympia said alright back to the matter at hand when are we going to Chicago? Darcy told her sister as soon as we get things back on track with you and your mother-in-law she has to be the one her with your children, and we are going to have to hire someone else to help her with the children while Douglas is working don't you think, Olympia agreed to what her sister was saying because she knew when they left going to Chicago tracking down Angel they were going to be gone for a while.

Two weeks later Darcy and Olympia was on their way to Chicago looking for angel they didn't have a clue that she wasn't in Chicago anymore Angel now resided in Missouri, when they arrived in Chicago the first thing they did was look up Ava and Denise just to let them know that they were back angel may have destroyed their physical being but their lives emotionally was back on track, mentally was a different story because mentally they were still having nightmares that torched them mentally on a regular basics.

But they knew getting in contact with Denise and Ava will open up a can of worms and just maybe they will tell baby girl that they were in town so she could either coming looking for them herself so they could beat her and disfigure her like her mother did them, right then a light switch popped on in Olympia's head she said you know what if we can't find angel let's just get the next best thing her precious baby girl I bet her crazy ass will walk across a burning pit to get her darling baby girl, so now the plan had changed they wasn't going to look up Ava and Denise they were going to stalk the trio to find out where they stayed and worked at instead, the whole trip was emotional for them but they had to keep their feelings under control just being in the presences of the Carter clan just bought back bad memories for the two of them.

They just felt the inner need to get back was stolen from them their self respect for themselves angel had to took a lot from them and they couldn't go on living their lives knowing she was out their living the life of an assassin and she could turn up anywhere and they didn't want to cross paths with her again without perfecting their skills against their enemy, Angel taught them how to kill people they were trained to shoot high powered weapons what worried them the most was why couldn't they catch the person they hated the most was dumfounded to them it baffled them a lot, but one thing they knew for sure was angel was on their shit list she had to be stopped.

Darcy and Olympia didn't know that angel son king was now living in Chicago he was running his drug empire to the fullest he had mad cash and soldiers that was very loyal to him, the last time they seen king he was a little boy know he was a grown man running shit in Chicago like he was the damn mayor, little did they know if they were coming after his sister they had to cross paths with the king, one way or the another he would be looking for them in every crack in the Chicago area, Darcy and Olympia had never been to Chicago they didn't know where to start they knew that baby girl was an attorney in Chicago so they decided there. Darcy and Olympia rented their room and fired up their laptop to find baby girl's location once they did their first step was done it was time to move on to step two which was stalking her they didn't know that Ava and Denise were partners with baby girl in her law firm what shocked them the most was the name of the law firm who came up with that name, what in the hell was they thinking, the name was K. A.W. A. which stands for kicking ass with attitudes they had a good laugh at the fact that they was so smart that they were really stupid.

That evening they went out for a bite to eat when they ran into an entourage of guys coming into the restaurant and they notice the leader of the gang looking in their direction, Darcy said look at that young guy smiling at me Olympia said I guess so sister we some fine ass sister baby girl, she said yes we are because Douglas was one hell of a surgeon and I would recommend him to anyone that has the same issue's that we had, now look at us it's all gravy we are the shit.

King walked over to their table to introduce himself to them because he was really feeling Darcy he didn't tell them his name was Ramon he never told anyone his government name he would always tell everyone his name was king, Darcy thought he was cute and funny as hell to her because she could crush his heart with all those curves on her body she was carrying around, but she decided to play his little game with him, he asked her was they from Chicago because of their southern accent and she told him no they were from Hawaii he said that's what I'm talking about Hawaii women is nice and brutal, Darcy said excuse me sweetie there isn't nothing nice about a woman scorned I don't care what breed she is player, king said oh I did your style "ma" so Darcy asked king if you don't mind where are you from? King said baby girl I'm from Columbia and I'm the king of Chicago now so this is where I will be into they put me six feet deep "you feel me".

Darcy was sitting there staring at king because her mind was trying to replace his face then it hit her in the stomach like diarrhea, she told her sister oh snap do you know who this young man is? She said no and how do you know him, but she didn't say anything about knowing king until he walked back to his table, Darcy told Olympia the king master sitting over there is angel little boy Ramon and that's going to be our way into the fold of their lives we are going to wreck havoc on them so bad until they gone ask us to stop.

Darcy found king and now it was on she told her sister I'm going to invite him back to our room not right now because we have to get another room two floors down so he won't know that we stay in the same hotel, then we are going to drug his young ass up and keep him tied up until we can plug in to his darling sister baby girl, she said I hear you loud and clear but how do you think we gone get his young ass alone when he travel with a group of soldiers, she told Olympia don't ever estimate your opponent because you as a female should know the power that we possess which is P.O.P. the power of the pussy.

King exchanged numbers with Darcy before him and his soldiers left the restaurant that evening, Dallas made sure to remind young king about his last encounter with someone older than him, king knew what he was saying was real talk but he just had a thing for older females so he was going to be more cautious with Darcy than he was with Skye.

King didn't have a clue that he was just a pawn in Darcy little web of deceit she wanted king to lead the way into his world of corruption, she knew how to seduce king young ass because his mother taught them seduction 101 when they killed the Sanchez brothers in Columbia, and soon young king will once again stick his foot in some shit because he can't keep his snake in his pants.

chapter thirty five
King Soldiers Getting Killed

King soldiers' had got into some beef with the other drug dealers on the south side of town by the time king received the call three of his soldiers was already dead, king, Dallas, Diego and Detroit was on their way to the south side when they pulled up in those black hummers bullets was been sprayed all over them who ever the nigga's was that was shooting at them had no idea that the hummers was bullet proof including the windows, by the time king and his right hand men started returning fire they heard police sirens getting closer to the scene where they were returning fire so they speed off in a different direction, king was pissed because three of his best soldiers was laid out in the ground full of holes how was he going to get to them without being detected.

King knew that he had to call pee wee sister Robin to tell her the bad news that her seventeen year old brother was dead, he also had to call strikers parents and McKee parents also and he knew it wasn't going to be nothing nice, but he was willing to pay for all three of their funerals because if nothing else they were loyal to him so he respected that, king wanted heads to roll on the killings of his soldiers, he didn't know what happen because he didn't answer the call when pee wee had called him to let him know that they were trying to rob them and they were under fire, he was at home in the nursery rocking his son to sleep while his phone was in the kitchen on the charger he didn't even hear his phone ringing he didn't even notice he had two missed call's.

When they made it back to king's condo he looked at his phone and noticed he had two missed calls when he heard pee wee's voice on his voice mail he broke down because he blamed himself for their deaths, if he had answered the phone the first two times maybe his soldiers wouldn't be laying up in the morgue with toe tags, he knew he had a lot to answer to from their parents and he wasn't ready to face them because how could he tell them that he was doing more for their son then they ever did without making them angry at the truth.

King had Dallas to drop twenty five thousand dollars off to each one of his fallen soldier's parents he thought that was more than enough and if they needed more he didn't have a problem sending more, he just felt responsible for what happen to his falling comrades in some kind of way he felt if he had of answered that called their deaths could of have been prevented, king was having trouble sleeping because now he had to replace the soldiers that he lost and that was going to be a hard task trying to find people he could trust, Dallas came up with the idea to tell king about the three guys he was in the joint with they were hard core killers like they was and he knew they could be trusted, king trusted Dallas with his life so if he could vouch for these three guys then it was worth looking into their background to find out about their history.

Dallas wanted king to feel safe with being in control with his empire and he wasn't about to invite know one into their fold that wasn't highly recommended by him, king told Dallas that if you 100 percent sure that these nigga's is gold than I'm with it but trust me when I tell you if them nigga's is foul I'm put two in their heads and that s real talk Dallas, Dallas told king young blood if they even look at you wrong I'm going to be in their assess like balled up toilet paper don't worry I got you my brother.

King loved Dallas and his brothers they were his godfathers he knew they wasn't there to harm him or let nothing happen to him, they was by his side the whole time so they knew young king was under pressure so to even out the drama he was dealing with Dallas decided if king would give his boy a chance at getting fed to in the drug business.

King told Dallas the next day that he decided to take him up on his offer he had baby girl to run checks on all three guys and found out who they were and where their families resided at so everything was a go, Dallas gave John boy, studs and ice a call and ask them how soon could they be in Chicago they told Dallas we can be there before day break, Dallas said cool and told them to give him a call when they touched down in Chicago, John boy called studs and ice to let them know it was a go they packed up an hour later and was headed to Chicago they touched down in Chicago at 4 am and called Dallas for directions to the hotel they was suppose to be staying at.

Dallas gave them directions to the hotel the only thing they had to do was rest because Dallas had already reserved their rooms and left their keys with the manger of the hotel at the front desk, when they went into their rooms all they could say was damn, Dallas had set them up in the Radisson hotel the rooms were big and nice and the fridge was stocked with whatever they wanted to drink including beer, John boy said damn my nigga Dallas must be doing the damn thing because I haven't been in nothing this nice ever.

The next morning about 8am Dallas was knocking on John boys door he was ready to take them to breakfast and meet young king, king didn't have trust in anyone without looking in their eyes first especially the kind of business he was running he didn't have patients for error, when Dallas arrived at the restaurant with his boys in tow they couldn't believe their eyes when they saw young king they all grunted like what the fuck this little nigga can't carry that much weight, Dallas told them I know why y'all thinking but don't let the size fool you because he's the man that's going to be giving y'all assess a chance to show him what y'all can do for real so don't let yawls mind over rule your assess alright, now sit down and let my man school y'all crazy assess, king looked each one of them in the eyes he told them what he expected from each one of them and they had to be loyal to him no matter what the situation was or wind up swimming with the fishes in the Mississippi river it was totally up to them he told them speak now or forever hold your peace.

John boy, studs and ice was in agreement with king even thou they didn't like the threat he had just made on their lives they went along with it because they knew one thing for sure if Dallas was involved him and his brothers this had to be some serious shit, after king gave them the details to the dope houses he wanted them to run he left the restaurant he dismissed himself from the table and headed home, but before he could pull out of the restaurant parking lot he remembered to tell Dallas to have them fitted for his electronic bracelets everybody

229

wore one but him and his brothers and that's because they had godfather status.

King made sure that Dallas kept a close eye on them for a while until he felt a little more comfortable with them running his south side dope house, he felt something wasn't right with them and to be safe with his product was better than being sorry later, Dallas said he understood where king was coming from and he would be closer to them than the underwear they were wearing, king laughed at Dallas because he knew that Dallas and his brothers was as loyal to him as they came and he wouldn't trade them in for all the gold in fort knoxs.

It had been two months and everything was working out fine until king had to go off on studs for being so careless he met a chicken head name Paris that ran a beauty shop on the corner she was so trifling talking about how she was in the sheets in front of every man that would listen, one day in particular when studs went down to the beauty shop to take her something to eat she was in the beauty shop talking to three guys, that was waiting on their barber to show up she was telling them how she can drop it like it's hot she even was demonstrating it in front of them rubbing all between her legs and shit, studs was so messed up behind what her trifling ass was doing he left the dope house door standing wide open when king and Dallas pulled up to check on the products studs wasn't nowhere to be found king was pissed at studs.

Dallas told king calm down player I told you I got this and Dallas knew where studs was he knew that trifling ass Paris had his nose wide open so finding him wasn't going to be a problem, when they looked up the street studs was coming up the street fuming Dallas didn't give a damn he grabbed studs around the neck and told him if he treasure his life he better not ever be caught leaving his post unattended again, Studs couldn't believe that Dallas grabbed him up like he was some chump he didn't know, he made a mental note to check Dallas when king wasn't around because he was a man first before he became this young nigga drug runner.

Dallas couldn't believe studs let Paris get under his skin like that because she had fucked every nigga in the hood everybody knew her as the hoe of the south side, so if a nigga was trying to run up in her ass it's because her body was tight and she had a good month piece on her, and that was so good even Dallas had to try it one night so he knew her mouth game was fire, Paris was a freak and everybody on the south side knew she was the F.B. I. A. the Freakiest Bitch IN America.

—•—

chapter thirty six

Baby Girl Getting Shot

— • —

Gloria (baby girl) was so sure of herself that she had started tripping she wasn't keeping her eyes on the ball lately that's how she got caught tripping by Skye's hired gun two time Tony, yes two time Tony got off two rounds in baby girl but she shot Tony three times he shouldn't have never trusted a pretty girl with a smile, he should have known that baby girl was as treacherous as he was, if anyone with common sense is holding a gun on you and their not begging for their own life but their looking you dead in the eyes like you're not a threat to them would you still be sitting there talking to this person like they're not as crazy as you are, that was two time Tony problem you don't have a conversation with someone you was sent to kill you do the job you was paid to do and move on.

Two time Tony didn't know baby girl was an assassin he only knew what Skye paid him to do and that was to take baby girl out of the equation, baby girl was shot twice but she was going to live she couldn't say that about two time Tony but she did know that Skye was behind her shooting and she was going to be dealt with very soon, when baby girl was rushed to the hospital she made sure she stayed conscious enough for them to contact Brooklyn and king to let them know she had been shot, when Brooklyn and king arrived at the hospital baby girl was in surgery, king called his mother angel to let her know what was going on and he told her not to worry he would give her details as soon as baby girl was out of surgery, Angel was worried to death about her daughter baby girl she knew she would be fine but that didn't stop her from wanting to go to Chicago to see how she really was doing for herself.

Baby girl was in surgery for three hours while they were carefully removing the bullets out of her arm and thigh the bullet in her thigh hit one of her main arteries causing her leg to bleed furiously, the doctors got the bleeding under control and baby girl was on her way to recovery she was so drugged she wouldn't of known if she was dead or alive, the doctors went out in the waiting area to tell king and Brooklyn that baby girl did good in surgery and that she will be asleep for a while in recovery but they could see her as soon as she wakes up. King asked the doctor where did his sister get shot at and was where she when it happen, the doctor told him that he didn't know that information and that the detectives will be up at the hospital soon to talk with them about what happen to baby girl, as soon as the doctor was leaving the waiting area detective Fox and detective Neal was getting off the elevator coming to ask the doctor about Gloria Carter, the doctor told them everything that he had told Brooklyn and King so the detectives had questions for king and Brooklyn as well, detective Fox was the first to speak to king and Brooklyn he introduced him and his partner and told them the details of the shooting he even told them that Tony Sharp was the guy that baby girl killed, detective Fox also told them that they did a background check on Tony and he had a criminal record a mile long and he also went by an alias name two time Tony, Tony Sharp had been on the most wanted list for two years every time they thought they were getting close to capture him he would disappear again without a trace.

King told the detectives that he better be glad my sister killed his ass because if she hadn't he would be looking down the barrel of my glock, the detective told king you can't go around making idle threats young man, king told detective Fox I don't make threats I make promise's, detective Fox told king you look like an intelligent young man I can only hope you're not out here in the streets stirring up trouble, king just looked at detective Fox like the gum shoe he was and said why would I be out here stirring up trouble my sister took care of his worthless ass didn't she, detective Fox said as far as we know it was self defense he was in her car and she was held at gun point and she fought back.

Detective Fox knew what king had on his mine he had met guys just like king in his day of being a police officer now that he was now a detective things had gotten worse he saw guys like king on a regular basic and he didn't trust any of them, so he was going to keep a closer eye on him for a while because the way it was told to him the whole Carter clan was dangerous people, king told detective Fox he didn't have anything more to say to them and if he wanted to talk with his sister when she woke up than he wanted to be present when he talked to her.

Detective Fox didn't know why king wanted to be present when they talked to his sister because she wasn't under arrest they just had to close the case, because to them two time Tony got what he deserved he had been hired to kill someone by a person that was now missing from the same hospital that baby girl was now in, once Brooklyn heard the detectives say missing he knew that Skye was out there somewhere still stalking him, king was in shock when he heard the name Skye he went ballistic he asked Brooklyn what do you know about Skye? He told king everything he knew and how dangerous Skye could be if you didn't do what she wanted.

Speaking of Skye she had that charm action going on the young officer that was posted up outside her hospital room door was digging her she knew it, and that was her way out of a bad situation she said to herself why not take advantage of prince charming he was always staring at Skye like she was stake dipped in gravy, that night Skye was having a bad nightmare screaming in her sleep when officer Robert came in the room to wake her out of her dream when she grabbed his gun and made him uncuff her, she hit officer Robert across the head with own revolver knocking him unconscious she puts on his uniform and leaves the hospital undetected.

King and Brooklyn knew they had to find Skye crazy ass especially now that baby girl wasn't able to defend herself against her, angel was on her way to Chicago knowing the police was hot on her trail she didn't care not when it came to her children she wasn't going to leave her daughter in the hospital alone without anyone watching her back, baby girl was gave a clean bill of health concerning her bullet wounds but she was still in a great deal of pain that's why the doctors kept her sedated, her son smoke haven't heard yet that his mother had been shot and king or Brooklyn wasn't in a hurry to tell him because he was so hot headed they didn't want him in the hospital acting a damn fool.

The next day Angel arrived in Chicago looking like a bag lady she was so heavy in disguise that the nurse's was asking her was she homeless, she even went as far as putting rotten dentures in her mouth she had on a grey raggedy wig, when she told the nurse that she had been sick for a couple of days and she came to the hospital to get a check up the nurse then informed her that they didn't wait on people that didn't have medical insurance, but she could go down the street to the free clinic they would wait on her without any insurance, angel told the nurse thank you and she asked if she could sit in the waiting area until she can catch her breath, the nurse said sure you can as long as you need to, While Angel was sitting there thinking of away to sneak into her daughters room she notice king and Brooklyn coming out of the room headed to the waiting area.

Angel sat quite in her chair sitting across from Brooklyn and king while they were talking about Skye and how they had to be careful and put one of kings soldiers on security watching baby girl, before angel could tell King who she was detective Fox walked in to the waiting area telling them that Skye had escaped and she was seen somewhere in the area of the hospital, angel said to herself that if this Skye person is after my daughter than she will be somewhere in this hospital the hospital morgue.

That same night baby girl woke up from her sedation she was having a dream that she was at home with her mother in Columbia, she couldn't remember what happen to her and why was she laying up in a hospital bed until she tried to move her arm and leg, she started to remember that some guy pulled a gun on her shot her twice and that's when she killed him but not before he told her that Skye was the one that hired him to kill her.

Three days later the doctor told baby girl she could go home the next following week she had started improving very quickly, when baby girl looked up and seen her son walking through the door she was happy to see him plus he had grown to except whatever she threw at him, smoke just didn't care anymore about the secrets of the family because he was thriving on making his own money and moving on to become the man everyone thought king was, so to be looked at as the outsider was going to be in his favor more sooner than later and baby girl will soon find out that smoke is going to be just like Jose warned her about him, being just like his father Jose drug dealer and rapist.

———————————— •◦• ————————————

chapter thirty seven

Angels Baby Brother

———————————•◦•———————————

Reginald angel's baby brother had finally finished his tour in the military, he thought as far as his father goes he was an only child he had no idea that his father was a rolling stone, he would soon find out that his father had more bastard children than the welfare system, what Reginald couldn't shake out his mind was the fact that the last time he seen baby girl she seems to think he looked like someone she knew, baby girl even asked him if his father's name was Cane Cantrell Carter, and once he told her she wasn't surprise, so now that he was out of the service it was time to dig up some dirt to find out if he has any living siblings besides the one's on his mother side of the family.

Reginald first step was to find baby girl to see what she knew that she hadn't told him that night at his mother fish fry, he could feel that she knew his father but how was a mystery to him, he didn't want to tell his mother what he was about to do because she shelter him his whole life and now it was time for him to step up to the plate, he had graduated from high school and went into the service right after graduation, Reginald knew deep down inside that he was carrying dark cloud over his head, he always knew his mother Mae wanted what was best for him, but the fact still remains that he got teased a lot growing up because he didn't look like his brother or his sister even thou his mother kept telling him they had the same father, Reginald couldn't hide the fact that he was taught how to become a man fighting for uncle Sam, he still had the knowledge to know that his mother would come up with money to him name brand clothing and shoes and she didn't have a job.

When Reginald was ten years old he remember how his mother used to dress up every Friday evening she would always be back home at mid-night, the next morning she would feed all three of them breakfast get them showered and dress for a day of shopping, he remember it going on for a couple of years because it all stopped when he was twelve, his mother never went out every Friday evening again, Reginald love his mother she was the sweetest mother a child could ask for, but Reginald knew his mother had her own Skelton's in the closet.

What bothered Reginald the most was the fact he didn't have that Jamaican accent that his mother and siblings had, he felt different he always did but he kept it under wraps, he needed answers now he wanted to know his father's family history, he didn't tell his mother what he found out before he went back to the service the night of the fish fry when he was home for two weeks, he also found out before he was done with his term in the service that he had a rare blood disease that needed medical attention fast he didn't think that he inherited from his mother, he found out that the disease had to hereditary from his father, hemolytic anemia is a term use to describe a group of rare, genetically transmitted blood disorders, that's the term the doctors in the military gave Reginald that s why he wants to know who is his father and if he has any sisters and brothers on his father side of the family.

When Reginald made it to baby girls law firm she was in her office talking with a client Reginald told the receptionist that he could wait because it was important that he talks with her today, he took a seat in the waiting area until baby girl was done with her client once she came into the waiting area and she seen it was Reginald she gave him a hug and they walked back into her office, Reginald didn't waste any time telling baby girl the events of the night at his mother s fish fry, he asked her did she remember asking him his father's name and she said yes I do, Reginald told baby girl l didn't come here for any trouble I need to know if you know my father I have a rare blood disease and I found out It was hereditary from my father, baby girl could only say she was sorry to Reginald but after he told her that he needed help right away she broke down and told him that his father was her grandfather and her mother Angel is his sister, Reginald sat there staring off in space because he really didn't know what to say, he asked baby girl did her mother stay in Chicago she said no but I can contact her for you maybe she can help you, but I do know that she don't know that you even exist because I haven't had the chance to tell her about you since the first night I met you at your mother's house, baby girl told Reginald I knew you were my uncle the first time I laid eyes on you because you and my mother look just alike, Reginald asked baby girl if she could give him Angels phone number so he could talk with her, baby girl told Reginald I can do better than that how about I set up a meeting with the two of you than you two can get to meet each other in person, but first I would have to tell my mother about you first because she doesn't take to kindly to people she doesn't know, Reginald said that would be fine here my number and I would look forward to hearing from you.

Baby girl knew she was going to open up a can of worms because Angel didn't give a damn about how many children her father had because in her eyes it was just her still living, all the other children her father had was all dead by her hands.

————— •●• —————

chapter thirty eight
Angel's Baby Daughter Keiasia

———————•❖•———————

Angel's baby daughter Keiasia is now five years she's growing up pretty quickly her father wants her to grow up to be a part of the family business her mother angel has other plans for her, Angel doesn't want her daughter to grow up the way that she did or her other children, she wants something better for her like being a doctor or whatever she wanted to be she didn't want her daughter to grow up running from the law like she was now doing, Angel looked back on her life and her children hoping she had of done some things different with baby girl and king now it was a lose cause because they were now as ruthless as she is and only time could tell what would happen to them in the long run.

Angel had set aside a lot of money for Keiasia so when she was old enough to go forward with her life she could go in the right direction of being the most valuable person she could be in this cruel world that she was growing up in, angel wanted to give her daughter something she never had a real chance to be a productive person in the environment that she lived in, even thou angel talked to her baby every day about the way the worlds turned she didn't understand what angel was saying she just said ok mommy and kept smiling, angel told her daughter baby when you complete circles don't allow squares because they don't fit, Keiasia just smiled again at her mother because she was only five years old she had no idea what her mother was talking about but her father did he enjoyed listening to angel talk to their daughter.

Ramon felt that angel had something brewing in that mind of hers because it was a everyday thing for her to talk with their daughter, but this time was different she had this strange look on her face that made him think she was up to something, angel asked Ramon what's wrong with you? Why you staring at me like that he told angel because I see you changing right before my eyes and I just want to know what's going on with you, she went on to tell Ramon that nothing was wrong she just wanted their daughter to succeed in life and have a better chance than they did, what's wrong with our daughter growing up with a positive attitude I mean I know it doesn't guarantee she will get the same from others but practice make perfect.

Ramon told angel its okay to make sure our daughter is happy but in order to do that we have to be happy to, I don't want our past to determine her future I want her to walk forward and to be careful in not looking back, I want our daughter to be the best at whatever she decides to do with her life I want her to know that her time is very precious and that our days come and go, and that she lives her life to the fullest as if it was her last because time doesn't wait on anyone it moves on.

Ramon agreed with Angel but he couldn't figure out what was going on in her head because she was talking and saying things he had never heard her say, Angel told Ramon I don't want to allow our daughter to have the same toxins of negativity we had put in our minds growing up she has a chance not to be ignorant like we were,

243

ignorance has no strength when it is ignored, I just want Keiasia to be happy there are still some things that are free and happiness is one of them, and sweet heart that's one to take advantage of.

Angel didn't want the chapter of her life catching up to her daughter Keiasia if it did she didn't want her to react on it she just wanted her to turn the page and keep moving forward, angel knew it was so many things in the world that was contagious she just wanted happiness and laughter be some of the things her daughter would catch, she also told Ramon that sometimes when opportunity knocks you have to look out before you let it in, not all opportunities are good some has a lifetime of regrets.

Ramon understood everything angel was saying because he felt her pain he also knew that she really did want what was best for their daughter Keiasia, the only thing angel was sure of was as long as she was still alive her daughter was going to be something she wasn't and that was as pure as the driven snow, angel knew one day the law was going to catch up with her or they may even kill her but she be damn if her daughter turned out to be like the rest of them she didn't want her to have to live in their shadows, Keiasia watched her mother and father sit at the kitchen table and talk she couldn't understand why they were talking so much about her but she would soon grow up to learn that the Carter family is not to be messed with on any level.

Angel had been home schooling Keiasia at home because she didn't want to have problems at school with anyone messing with her daughter so she went to every store she could find to get everything she needed to home school her daughter, what angel didn't know that it was alright with home schooling Keiasia but she was taking her out of an environment to function with other children her own age, Ramon asked angel what was really going on because even thou her mouth was saying one thing her mind was telling him something else.

Angel told Ramon I'm just getting her ready for what's about to happen because I'm either going to get caught by the law one day or I might just turn myself in because I'm really getting tired of watching my back everywhere I go, Ramon made a statement to angel if you do that what's going to happen to our daughter because if the law gets you they will have me as well because we are in this together don't ever forget that, Angel was most definitely thinking one sided because she didn't think Ramon would go as far as she did in turning herself in if she decided to do so.

Angel looked at Ramon and said right now is not an option we both have to make sure our daughter is old enough to take care of her, so there's no need for us to be thinking about anything else but Keiasia for now so let's just drop all this crazy talk for now.

Keiasia was sitting on the floor playing with her baby doll looking up at her parents she didn't know what was going on but she was very interested in what they were saying even thou she didn't understand none of it right now.

---

chapter thirty nine
Angel Going To Chicago

Angel received a call from baby girl saying that she needed to see her in person angel wanted to know was something wrong but baby girl assured her she was doing fine she was out of the hospital and was back at work, angel told baby girl that she would be there the next day because they were only three hours away and her sister would love to see her big sister and brother, angel didn't know that baby girl had a surprise for her but she would soon find out that she had one remaining relative left.

Angel, Ramon and their daughter Keiasia arrived in Chicago that after none she called baby girl to let her know that they had just checked in at the new precise hotel on the out skirt of Chicago, she asked baby girl could she come to the hotel after work and she said sure she would be there angel asked her if she would bring king and little cane with her, baby girl said she would but she was also bringing someone else to that she thought her mother should meet as well.

Angel didn't feel right being in Chicago she had this warm feeling come over her that made her break out in a heavy sweat she knew something wasn't right, but in her heart she felt that she was being watched and she had only been in town for a couple of hours before she called her daughter to let her know of her arrival, while angel was on the other side of town letting her mind play tricks on her baby girl was calling her uncle Reginald to let him know that his sister had made it to town, Reginald was glad to finally see that baby girl kept her word that she could get her mother to come to Chicago but Reginald didn't have a clue to how dangerous his sister really was.

Baby girl told Reginald when she picked him up that she still hadn't told her mother about him she just thought that if she seen him in person she would know that he was her brother just like she did when she first saw him, baby girl called and asked king to pick up her son and for them to meet her at the square on the out skirt of Chicago, that was a code word for whenever they would talk on their phones to each other that would let king know their mother was in town.

King knew what the square was he also knew it meant by his apartment the square was two blocks from king's apartment, king had arrived at the square him and smoke was sitting there when baby girl and this guy pulled up, king said alright big sis I know you tripping now who the hell is this nigga? she said I know you haven't never seen our grandfather neither have I nothing more than a picture but look at this picture than look at him and then tell me what you think, king couldn't say shit because he knew who ever this guy was he was a spitting image of his mother so he had to be related but how, king didn't have anything else to say he just wanted to see how his sister was going to represent this nigga to their mother.

When baby girl arrived at the precise hotel she was the first one to get out of the car she wanted to go in first to make sure the close was clear before she bought her uncle into the room where her mother was, baby girl knocked on the door and Ramon answered the door he was standing there while Keiasia hold on to his leg she had grew up pretty quick in four years time to baby girl, baby girl asked Ramon where was her mother he told baby girl she's in the shower she should be out in a minute, baby girl said alright we will be outside waiting in the car until she gets dressed can you have her to call my cell when she comes out and get dressed please, Ramon said sure and baby girl went back outside to the car to let everyone know that she was in the shower, once angel got dressed she called baby girl to let her know she was out of the shower and that they needed to come on in, baby girl and smoke walked in first and king and Reginald walked in behind them when Reginald stepped from behind king angel eyes bucked open real wide she said out loud it couldn't be, it was like looking into a mirror Reginald look more like their father Cane than any of his children he had Canes face, body and swagger he even sound like him to angel, angel asked Reginald if they could talk in private because she wanted to know everything about him to where he was born to who is his mother was.

Angel took Reginald down stairs to the bar area of the hotel she was happy she had a brother still living but she also didn't trust the fact that he was just now coming out of the woodwork what was his reason and why now, Reginald looked at angel he told her I didn't come here to start any trouble nor did I come here for a family reunion I found out while I was in the service I have a rare blood disorder and I was told It was heredity from my father I was looking for relatives that was still living on my father side of the family so I could get a background family history, angel told Reginald I'm sorry but our father was killed when I was five years old I never knew him and he only had one brother that I knew but he 's also dead I killed him myself for molesting me when I was a child, When she said that Reginald did a double take because he never met someone that was bold enough to admit to murder.

Angel saw the way Reginald was looking at her and she said don't be shocked baby brother that bastard deserved everything I did to him, because he shouldn't have touched me I was a baby and he took something that was precious and turned me into a demon from hell, Reginald couldn't do anything but sympathize with angel because if he had a daughter he would have killed him to for molesting his daughter, but he could see that angel had the same killing instincts he had but he was trained by the military for the killings he had done, but his sister looked like a one woman killing machine he even notice that when angel bent over she was strapped with two 9mm on her side, Reginald asked angel if she knew of any more male son's that their father may have had that's still living angel told Reginald I have to keep it real with you we don't have any more siblings living at all our father had four other son's and a daughter and I killed all of them lying ass—holes.

Reginald was took by surprise with what angel had just said because he couldn't believe she killed everyone of their siblings and she didn't hesitate to tell him that she murdered them without even blinking her eyes, angel told Reginald I'm sorry for you having a blood disease but you are going to have to fine help somewhere else because the only two people left in the Carter clan is you my brother and my children and they have been cleared of anything containing to a blood disease, Reginald asked angel was she sure it had to be some kind of way she could help him he was fighting for his life and he wasn't about to give up without a fight, angel told Reginald I wish I did know of a way but I don't I told you that we are the only ones left.

Reginald told angel thanks anyway but he knew he had to do some research on the rare blood disease he had it has to be a doctor out there that can save his organs from shutting down, angel really did feel sorry for her brother but she felt it wasn't her problem to help him because no one in the family reached out to help her so why should she play captain save a hoe, you could see in angel's eyes that she admired the fact that she did have a little brother left that wasn't trying to bring harm to her or her family he was only trying to get some answers to his family history.

What touched angels heart the most about seeing her brother he was most defiantly Canes son he couldn't lie his way out of that one if he tried because Reginald look like Cane carried him himself, angel and her brother went back into her hotel room and when baby girl looked at her uncle it didn't seem like he had gotten any answers from her mother, he was still carrying that worried and concerned look on his face, baby girl asked angel what she thought of her brother? Angel said what do you mean yes he is my father's son is that what you mean, baby girl told her mother he is the only sibling you have left mother he could be good for you but you have to bond with him first, you know some of the things that you preach about to me and king you need to practice what you preach.

I think you should give Uncle Reginald a chance you will be surprise what you might find out he's different than the rest of us mother he's really a special guy I like him, give him a chance to prove his worth, before you turn on him he wants to be a part of this family can't you tell, no what I see is a young man looking for his father for answers to save his life, look baby girl I'm not as heartless as you may think I 'm going to find someone to help him I just didn't tell him yet, I need to find the doctors that knows his condition before I let him know that I'm helping him first, baby girl was happy to see that her mother wasn't the vicious person that she grew up watching even thou she never mistreated her she was grateful for having angel as her mother, all she wanted was for her mother to experience brotherhood with her brother like baby girl had been doing with king she felt her mother needed her brother just as much as he needs her.

chapter fourty

Angel's Retirement

---•◦•---

Angel had been feeling like her life wasn't what she wanted it to
be lately she had been second guessing herself every turn she was
making, it was like god was telling her it was time for her to repent
she had gotten older now and her time on earth was winding down
either she was trying to escape the law or running from state to state
trying to fit in somewhere, angel had more to think about now she
had her daughter Keiasia to think about now she thought if she
turned herself in she could spend the rest of her life behind bars but
if she was to get into another shoot out with the police she could
get killed, she didn't want to just give up her life in exchanged for
some bars and an orange jump suit she wanted to stay out of jail long
enough to see her daughter grow up graduate from high school and
go off to college.

Angel knew she had a lot of demons to face but she didn't have any
remorse for anything she had done she had been lied to and abused
by men her whole life so in her mind she wasn't regretful for what
she had done to the men she came across in her life as an assassin, she
knew deep down inside that she had the power to change the course
of her life now if not for herself for her baby daughter, she had the
urge to tell Ramon what she was thinking but she decided against it
for now because she really wasn't sure how she wanted to approach
the situation herself first.

Angel needed time to think her thoughts through before she came to terms with her retirement she wasn't sure what she wanted to do, but she did know one thing for sure that she didn't want to get caught up in a shoot out again with the police or the feds because it will be more bloodshed this time and it wasn't going to be hers, angel happen to be sitting in her window one morning and she got hit with a thought of when she was five years old, what happen to her at that aged she had blocked out of her mind but it return to her like a flashback she could see her uncle coming into her room and sliding under the covers with her, he started playing with her little kitty cat like she was a grown women he also made her do oral sex on him forcefully she would cry herself to sleep, when her parents would finally come pick her up at night she would always be fully dressed asleep on the couch.

Angel didn't have a second thought of killing her uncle she sent him away in a blaze of glory she found an empty gas can and took it to the gas station and had an old man that was standing around the gas station to go and buy her two dollars worth of gas, when she returned back to her uncle's house he was drunk asleep on the couch she poured gas all over the couch and her uncle she found his cigarette lighter and she lit the lighter and threw it on top of her uncle, she watched him roll around on the floor trying to put himself out but he didn't have any luck he was burning as fast as a forest in the San Diego hills, what bother her at the time she went and got the gas from the gas station that the man that was hanging around the gas station didn't ask her not one time why a little girl at the age of eight years old wanted to but some gasoline.

Angel had suffered from the hands of her uncle molesting her from
the time she was five until she was eight years old she tried to tell
her parents what was going on but her father refuse to believe that
his brother was molesting his baby girl, not only did she get played
by her uncle putting his grubby hands on her but her brother ST.
Louis got her pregnant and set her up to go to jail with her sister the
prosecuting attorney Isabel Stallone, angel started reminiscing about
her life she had been beaten, drugged up and raped she had even been
shot.

She knew she wasn't a saint she had her share of abuse and all kinds of
tragedy so what she did to other people was what she was taught and
trained to do, she knew before she finally closed her eyes she would
see everything she did in her life that was detrimental to everyone that
was involved, angel wanted to set things straight in her life she knew
she couldn't bring back the people she killed and she didn't want to
because some of them deserved what she did to them, she felt that
she was betrayed by a lot of people including the people she thought
that loved her and was her family the Salvador's for one was suppose
to be her family, but when she found out that they had betrayed her
and killed her parents she could only see blood and angel felt the only
way she could be free of the lie's was to bring down the whole family
including her brothers David and Dante.

Angel felt it was time to free her heart of all the killings she wanted
to be able to sleep at night without the demons, but before she
retired she had to set things in motion with uncle Leo first before
she told Ramon what she wanted to do, she still wanted to be their
Columbian assassin one day but right now she had other things on

her plate so she wanted to hang up her weapons for a while, she felt that if it was really necessary she will come out of retirement later but right now she think it will be better if she pass's being assassin over to her daughter baby girl she is more than equip to walk in her angel's shoes plus she has the stigma to keep it going, but if baby girl was ever in a bind angel would be there to watch her back without a doubt in her mind, angel talked to uncle Leo about her retirement and he wished her good luck and he told her if she ever wanted to come back her job will be waiting on her, he also agreed that baby girl would be a good choice she moved in the night like a ninja like her mother so they both knew she could handle the job.

Uncle Leo hated the fact that angel wanted to retire but he knew she would come back one day because he knew killing was all she knew, after angel talked things out with Uncle Leo her retirement was final she told Ramon that night that she decided to retire just for a while and that she and Uncle Leo thought that baby girl would work out just fine.

Angel had walked her daughter down to the store to buy her a candy apple when she saw this guy pulling this little girl into an empty building, all the molestation that she had been through in her life resurfaced right then she watched how the man put his hand over the little girls mouth to keep her quite, angel asked the clerk in the store would she watch her daughter right quick while she run back home to get her money to pay for the candy apple, the clerk say sure, angel had the money in her pocket she just didn't want that little girl living with the fact that some man took something from her that didn't belong to him, and living with the fear that all men were animals like she had been thinking until she met Ramon, all angel could think about was one for the road then she would be retired for a while but she couldn't let that man getting away with molesting that little girl or worse.

Angel had her 9mm tucked under her jacket when she entered the empty building the man had already knocked the little girl out cold he had ripped he underwear off and was about to enter her with his penis until angel said in a whisper move and I will blow your head off, the man turned around and looked at angel with blood shot eyes, he said bitch you don't know me this here is my niece I'm trying to teach her ass a lesson, when angel heard him say niece it sent her back into time when her uncle molested her she told the man wrong answer mister, she shot the man four times her last shot took his penis right off and it landed on the floor right next to his dead corpses.

Angel saved that little girl that day from all the bad memories she would have had if that man had of got away with raping her, angel flagged down a cab that was passing by and paid the cab driver to take her to the hospital the cabbie asked what was wrong with her and angel told him she didn't know she found her unconscious, the cabbie took the fifty dollars and drove the little girl to the hospital like he was told to do, when the cabbie arrived at the hospital with the little girl she had finally came to she was able to tell the emergency doctors about the man that tried to rape her but she didn't really remember anything else after that, the cab driver was able to give the police a detail description of the woman that asked him to drive the little girl to the hospital he was even ready to show them where the lady flagged him down at if they needed to go look at that empty building.

The doctors did an exam on the little girl she was find angel got to her on time they also was able to reach the little girl's mother, the little girl was nine years old her mother would let her walk to the corner store from time to time by herself, and the man that tried to rape the little girl really was her crack head uncle that angel killed, but one thing for sure he wouldn't be trying that shit again ever not in this life time he won't.

———— •●• ————

chapter fourty one

10 Questions About The Book:

—— •◦• ——

1: Is baby girl really going to be a good assassin for the Columbian mafia?

2: Do you think angel will come out of retirement sooner than later?

3: will king ever get caught running drugs out of king towers?

4: will Kaylen and Keith remain loyal to king or will they try to kill him?

5: what do you think should happen to Skye?

6: Baby girl son smoke will she ever find out about smoke being in the

Family business?

7: Is Angel ever going to marry Ramon?

8: Darcy and Olympia will they ever find angel and make her pay for

Killing their mothers?

9: Ava and Denise will they finally find true love?

10: Will Conner come back and wreck havoc on the Carter clan?

WILL ANGEL COME OUT OF RETIREMENT TO SAVE HER SON WAIT AND SEE IN BOOK #4 COMING SOON! ANGEL A HUSTLING DIVA WITH A TWIST CONTINUES!

About The Author

BRENDA (GEAN) Wright was born and raised in St. Louis, MO. Her greatest accomplishments were opening up her own DAYCARE CENTER. She grows up without her mother who passed away when she was twelve years old.

Her father also deceased. She graduated from Sumner high school. She went on to college and took up medical assistant and furthers her education in childcare. She's happily married to her husband (William) for fifteen years. She has two children (CHRISTINA) and (JAMES), two step children (ORLANDO) and (RESHUNDA) she has ten grandchildren and six brothers and two sisters. When she's not keeping children she spends her time writing in her laptop, her hobby is baking cakes and cookies for her grandchildren and for sale. Right now she's in the process of going back to school for her Masters Degree in Business Administration